Phyllis
Almeta
Smith

Rated XX.
Several Type's
in this book!
Hot Pleasure
Reading!

TURNED OUT

TURNED OUT

ANGEL M. HUNTER

www.urbanbooks.net

Urban Books
10 Brennan Place
Deer Park, NY 11729

ISBN-13: 978-0-7394-8313-8

Printed in the United States of America

Dedicated to my family
Only they can handle me.

Dedicated to my husband
Tony B. Irby
Thanks for allowing me to be myself and giving me the most precious gift in life, our son, the future poet, Anthony S. Irby.

Dear Friends:

I want to thank you for accepting my storytelling. In my writings, I try to address issues that everyday people face and these issues change often. Issues such as sexuality, drug use, racism, abuse and spirituality.

Sometimes people are afraid to reveal what's going on in their lives, afraid to voice their feelings and expose what they consider secrets, for fear of being judged.

From e-mails and letters I've received, I realize that a lot of people want to live out loud, share and know that they have options and choices. Please know that you are not alone in your internal and external struggles. There's always someone going through what you're going through, or who's been through it already. We must support one another.

I thank you for your continued support and your words of encouragement. Keep reading!

Angel M. Hunter-Irby

I would also like to thank Carl Weber and Roy Glenn for believing in my writing. Thanks for "getting it." I'd also like to thank Arvita Glenn for pushing me along.

Thoughts of Tracy, Sharon, Aisha, and Selena.

CHAPTER ONE
"SHINING STAR"
EARTH, WIND & FIRE

At the age of 29, you would think Champagne Rose had it all. She worked as a publicist in New York City and was engaged to the man of many women's dreams, Zyair Truesdale. Not only was he a wealthy entrepreneur, but he was kind, supportive, and willing to do anything for her. Even with the picture-perfect life, Champagne felt that something was missing, and she was ready to make changes in her life and in her relationship.

She didn't believe in moving in with someone before marrying them, up until Zyair convinced her otherwise. Now five years later, she and Zyair still lived together, unmarried.

The funny thing was, he wanted to get married, but she was comfortable with what they had. She enjoyed having her own bank account. She enjoyed the independence that came with not being married. Champagne watched her friends' relationships fall apart right after they got married, for one reason or another, and didn't want that to happen to her and Zyair.

She wasn't ready to get married, but she also wasn't ready to break up. It's just that they'd been together now for so long and things were starting to wear thin. The chemistry just wasn't there. The sex had become routine, the same shit over and over—You lick me, I suck you, you put it in, and then I'll ride you. You come, and I'll come, maybe . . . if I'm lucky. At least that's how she perceived it.

Champagne yearned for more caressing, kissing, cuddling, and talking. She knew she still loved him, but the passion was gone. She often found herself avoiding sex altogether.

If it was bothering her, it had to be bothering him. Was it her? Was it him? Was it their busy lifestyles? Whatever it was, she knew it had to change, and fast. She wanted to feel his fingers in her hair, moving down to her neck, where his fingers would be replaced with his lips. She wanted him to tease her with his tongue, tease her with his manhood, putting just the tip in and pulling it out. She wanted to beg for it, to demand that he enter her. She was tired of him putting it in, whether she was ready or not, tired of the roll-over sex, the moving-in-and-out, up-and-down momentum of it all. She was just plain tired.

Champagne wanted things to change. She needed things to change. She still loved him, for goodness' sake. She just wasn't in love. *Were you supposed to stay in love*, she wondered, or did this happen to every couple? If it did, the thought frightened her. She was determined to gain back what they once had.

Sometimes late at night as they made love, she would lay in their king-sized bed and let her mind wander. She pretended to instruct him, tell him what to do, where to kiss. She'd ask him if he forgot her secret spots, and he would then ignite the slowly fading fire.

She chose to hold these thoughts in. She realized thinking something and saying it were two different things. She was afraid. She didn't want to hurt his feelings, and she definitely didn't want him going off to be with some other woman, just to prove he still had it.

So she put up with the mediocre sex and wondered if he was doing the same.

Little did she know, Zyair was getting bored with their sex life as well. The fireworks and the umph was gone. It wasn't like he wasn't attracted to Champagne anymore. He was. To him, she was still fine and sexy. He was still drawn to her, still interested. Heck, he was ready to marry her. So why wasn't their sex life the way it used to be? Why wasn't it as intense as it used to be? He remembered when they used to have to dry their bodies off because of the steam they created together.

They used to have sex in every room, and everywhere. She'd even given him a blowjob in the car not once or twice, but a number of times. Now he could count the number of times she'd suck his dick in a month—on one hand. What the hell was going on with them? He wished he had the answer.

Sometimes while they were making love, he would feel his dick go soft. He would then have to close his eyes and fantasize. Normally, that fantasy included another woman. *So common*, he thought, but he couldn't help it. He didn't have this fantasy because he wanted to sex someone else down. He did because he believed it would enhance what was slowly fading. He also knew it was an ego thing. He wanted to be "the man," the one to satisfy two women. He also wanted to see his woman being pleased. He loved how she looked when she was at the point of no return, the way her eyes would close and her mouth would part, and she would arch her back and let out a soft moan.

The other reason was because, honestly, his mind did stray and he did think about new pussy every now and again, and this way he could actually get it without cheating. So, on second thought, maybe he did want to sex another woman down.

Just like Champagne, he didn't say anything. He didn't want her to kick him out or kick his ass. She might even have accused him of having an affair, which wasn't the case. That was in the past, where it belonged. He'd been there, done that, got caught, and won't do it again.

Zyair Truesdale owned his own business. Well, actually it used to be his parents', and when they'd retired, they turned it over to him. Both parents were now deceased. His father had died four years earlier of a heart attack, and his mother less than a year later, of heartache. At least, that's what he believed.

Being the educated brother he was, he capitalized on it in a big way. Because of his business sense, Zyair was able to live comfortably. He thanked his parents in his prayers and knew they would've been proud of him and what he'd done with the business.

Private Affairs, an upscale restaurant and catering service, had two locations, one in New Jersey, the other in Georgia. His plan was to open a third in Miami within the next two years. Only the rich or well-off could afford the prices, and that's how Zyair wanted to keep it. The food was not only delectable, but the ambiance was classy. And on Thursday through Sunday, he showcased live bands.

*   *   *

It was where Zyair and Champagne met. She was wining and dining one of her potential clients, Jackson Davis, an up-and-coming actor who'd just landed a movie with top-billing stars, and he was looking for someone to get his name and face out there. He'd heard that Champagne was the one.

Jackson was flirting with her, trying to get the message across that he was interested in more than business, but she pretended like she didn't notice.

From across the room, Zyair couldn't take his eyes off her but didn't want to say anything, not knowing if they were on a date. It was obvious that the gentleman she was with wanted more than she was willing to give. Every now and then, he would try to take her hand, and she would pull back. He'd lean in a little close, and she'd lean away. Zyair chuckled to himself. "Damn, brother, can't you take a hint?"

Finally, Champagne stood up to go to the ladies' room.

Zyair saw this as his opportunity. He walked a short distance behind her, and paced a short distance from the bathroom door, waiting for her to come out.

When she stepped out and started heading towards her table, he approached her. "Excuse me, are you and your date enjoying your meal?"

Champagne placed her hands on her hips and playfully asked him, "Are you a restaurant critic or something?"

Laughing, he told her he was the owner of the establishment and was just checking on his most attractive customer.

Flattered, Champagne smiled. She liked the fact that he was straight to the point. She had noticed him watching her and already knew who he was. After all, she worked in the public relations field, and it was her business to know everyone with status, especially in the African-American community.

A month earlier, she went out to lunch with Alexis, her best friend since college. She'd just read a feature article on him in *Black Enterprise* and was impressed. After showing his picture to Alexis, she joked, "This man is fine as hell. Rich and smart. I'm fine, going to be rich, and bordering on brilliant. Don't you think we'd make a good couple?"

Alexis laughed. Little did she know, that prediction might be coming true. Would she laugh when she heard that she might stand a chance?

"Well," Zyair said, interrupting her thoughts, "are you and your date having a good time?"

"He's not my date, he's a client. And, yes, we're having a good time." Champagne glanced towards the table and noticed Jackson looking their way.

"I have to get back."

"What's your name?"

"Champagne Rose."

"Really?"

"Yes, really."

Placing her right hand in his, he brought it to his lips and placed a soft kiss on it. "Well, Champagne Rose, can I call you or see you again?"

Looking him in the eyes and shaking on the inside, Champagne said, "How about I call you?"

"You don't know my name or my number."

"Zyair Truesdale," she told him, "and I'll call you here." On that note she walked away and left him with a smile.

"She knew who I was all along," he said to himself. He liked a woman that played hard to get.

Sometimes Champagne would think back to that moment and recall the rush of talking to him the first time. She wished they could go back and start all over again. Maybe not all over, because they'd overcome a lot and some things she didn't want to repeat. What she did want a repeat of was the energy of a new relationship. Realistically, she knew it was too late for that, but it wasn't too late to make some kind of change.

CHAPTER TWO
"LET'S WAIT AWHILE"
JANET JACKSON

Champagne was irritated by the waiter's rudeness and intended on telling him so. Then again, maybe she was just on edge considering she and Zyair were out to dinner to have "a talk," the two most dreaded words in a relationship.

Lately they'd been having a lot of disagreements about nothing and at the most inopportune times. Sometimes it would start first thing in the morning, putting a damper on the rest of her day and leaving her unable to focus and with her mind racing.

Zyair would be doing the same.

Each would think of what they should have said or how they could have handled the situation better. If the disagreement wasn't first thing in the morning, it was right before bedtime, leaving them unable to sleep, but faking it for fear another disagreement would start up.

Everything one of them did seemed to irritate the other. It didn't matter what it was, from leaving the plate on the table, to leaving the toilet seat up, or talking loud on the phone. There was entirely too much tension in the house, and it was time to bring it to a head.

Earlier that day, fed up with the nonsense, Champagne suggested they go out to dinner to "talk and discuss some things."

Zyair agreed, figuring it would be an opportunity to get some things off his chest as well. He was ready to get out of this rut they were in and move forward.

They sat at the Soul Africana café, having cocktails and waiting on their appetizers.

"So," Zyair said, making a weak-ass effort to break the ice.

"So?" Champagne replied.

Zyair loosened his tie. "What's on your mind?"

Champagne took a deep breath. "I feel like our relationship is at a standstill. I feel like it's taken a turn for the worst, like something is missing, like we're stuck in a place I don't want to be in. I don't want to continue feeling this way, and I need to know if you're feeling the same way." There she'd said it. Now all she had to do was wait on his response.

For a moment Zyair didn't respond. He'd suspected what this talk would be about, but for her to blurt it out, putting it out in the air that way took him off guard. He wondered if it was his fault or whether they were both to blame. He knows that it takes two to make or break a relationship. Was theirs broken or in need of slight repair? "I agree," he told her. "So what do you propose?"

Since he agreed, Champagne wondered why didn't he bring this up before she did, and how long he'd been holding back.

"I don't know. Maybe a vacation, maybe counseling, maybe time apart."

"Time apart?"

That threw Zyair for a loop. Why would they need time apart? A relationship can't be fixed with time apart, you needed to be together to make it work. Maybe what she really was saying is that she wanted to break up? Damn, could that be it? Could that be the real reason behind this talk? He didn't want that. Despite their differences, he couldn't imagine growing old with anyone else. That whole getting out there, meeting new people, learning their quirks, their likes and dislikes was a lot of work, and he had enough work on his plate. He'd had his share of gold-diggers and wasn't ready to experience the drama again.

"Time apart? How is time apart going to help us?"

"I suggested more than time apart, and if you felt the same way why didn't you say anything?"

"Honestly . . . because I didn't know what to say. I couldn't pinpoint what was wrong."

"But you knew something was?"

Zyair sighed and reached across the table, and Champagne placed her hand on top of his. "Yes, Champagne, I did. Listen, I don't know what you want me to say. I don't have any solutions, but I do know that time apart is not what we need. Maybe what we do need is time together on some exotic island, away from the pressures of work and other outside sources."

Before Champagne could say anything, the waiter returned, placed their appetizers on the table, and walked away. Didn't even ask if they needed anything else.

Champagne tried to pull her hands away to call the waiter over, but Zyair, knowing how she was about service, squeezed her hands. "What do you think the problem is?"

"I don't know either. I just feel like things have gotten routine, and that we got too contented."

"Contented? You say that like it's a bad thing." He removed his hands.

"I'm not saying that at all. What I'm saying is, sometimes I wish we still had that I-can't-wait-to-see-you-and-want-to-be-around-you-every-minute-of-the-day anticipation we had when we first got together."

"Champagne, is that realistic?"

"Probably not, but the thought is nice."

Zyair smiled because he remembered that feeling like it was yesterday, the anxiety of the first phone call one week after their initial meeting at Private Affairs. Thoughts of her overwhelmed him, and he just couldn't stop thinking about her. He wondered if she would call or if she just played him.

Right when he'd given up hope, she called. He was unavailable at the moment, busy going over a contract with the new chef, and told his assistant to tell her he would call her back within the hour.

"Zyair?" she asked, when he said hello into the phone.

"How did you know it was me?"

"You're unforgettable," she flirted. It was because of caller ID and the fact that his voice and his lips were unforgettable. She remembered thinking after the short conversation they had, *You could fall in love with those full, luscious lips*, lips that were made for kissing, and the same lips that kissed her hand.

"I'm glad you called. For a minute there I was giving up all hope," he told her.

After leaving the restaurant that day, she thought of him often. She wished she had given him her cell phone number instead of taking his. She wondered if it made her seem to aggressive. Back and forth she debated. Should I call him or not. What will I say? Will he ask me out, or will we just flirt? Lack of confidence, then doubt, kept her from picking up the phone.

"Girl, call the man," Alexis told her when she expressed her fear, "Remember, he asked you if he could see you again."

"Yeah, you're right." Champagne dialed the number, full of anxiety and feeling like a child about to go the candy store, only to be told he'll call her back within the hour. She tried her hardest not to watch the clock but found herself doing it anyway.

"So how's your week been?" he asked.

"I've just been busy trying to make a dollar." Champagne said.

"You're a publicist, right?" He'd done his research. That's one of the perks of being rich. You can find out almost anything about anyone. He knew he was wrong for having her investigated, but before he took someone out or got too involved, he had to know a little bit about them.

Champagne didn't recall telling him. "Yeah. How did you know that?"

He lied, "One of my waiters recognized you. He worked an event for one of your clients."

She tried to recall his staff and couldn't. "Oh."

"Would you like to go out sometimes?"

She thought he would never ask. "Sure. When?"

"Tomorrow around seven p.m. We could do dinner and perhaps a show."

"I'd like that."

They chatted for a short while longer and agreed to meet at Private Affairs and leave from there. Champagne wasn't ready for him to know where she lived.

That first date was like a fairytale. He had a limo waiting outside for them.

"You go all out for all your dates?" Champagne asked, not really caring because she was the one getting the special treatment tonight.

"No, I wanted to impress you," he told her honestly. "I also didn't want to have to concentrate on driving. I wanted all my attention to be on you."

Damn, a brother was smooth and fine.

Every date after that, they looked forward to with excitement. Maybe it was the newness of it all, getting to know one another, or the anticipation of the love-making they both determined would come sooner rather than later. It could have been the fact that when they met, they were both looking for someone to share their lives with and found it in each other.

Whatever it was, it had up and disappeared, and it was now time to address the issue.

"Let's take this opportunity and discuss the pros and cons of our relationship," Zyair suggested.

Champagne rolled her eyes. "This isn't about business, this is about us. Our relationship. Pros and cons? What kind of mess is that?"

"Well, you're the one who said you wanted to talk."

"I do."

"Well, I was just making a suggestion."

"Well, make another one."

Zyair sighed. "Okay, let's do it this way. You say one thing that needs to change or has been bothering you, and I'll do the same."

"We can't get mad at each other either, okay," Champagne said, not wanting this to turn into something ugly.

"I agree. This is about bettering us as a couple, not breaking each other down as individuals."

"Okay, I'll go first," Champagne volunteered. "Maybe we've gotten bored with one another."

"Bored? I don't know if that's it. Maybe we've gotten more like routine. Everything is the same. It's stagnant, our work schedules, what we do when we get home, even the sex."

"The sex?" Champagne panicked. She knew it and wanted to be the first to address it, but to hear him say it brought up all sort of insecurities.

"Why are you picking up on that one thing? You're the one who said we wouldn't get offended or anything."

"I know you're right. It's just that—never mind. You're also right about the sex thing."

It was now Zyair's turn to be offended. "Are you saying I don't please you?"

"Are you saying I don't please you?"

They just looked at one another, Champagne thinking of him straying, Zyair wondering how many orgasms she's faked.

Champagne broke the silence. "You please me, Zyair. It's just that we barely kiss, we barely touch. You just go right for the gusto." *Even when you do that, I'm not wet enough. And when you to go down on me, you act like it's not something you want to do. You just go straight for the clitoris. Whatever happened to licking around, tasting every inch of it?* Champagne thought to herself. There was no way she was going to say that part out loud.

Zyair frowned. "The reason we don't kiss is because you turn your head. The reason we don't touch is because you're always tired. And the reason I always go for the gusto is because I thought that's what you wanted." *Plus, you barely suck my dick. I feel like I have to force-feed you, and when you take it upon yourself, you just lick it and put the head in. You don't devour it like you used to.*

"I guess we're both to blame for what's happened to us." Champagne tried to recognize.

"Yeah, I guess we are. So the question remains, What are we going to do about it?"

Champagne cleared her throat. "I have some suggestions."

"Go ahead."

"Let's make one day a week our date night. We have to do something together outside the house, something we normally wouldn't do."

"Like?"

"Take dance lessons, go to a play. We haven't done that in a while. Let's try a new restaurant. We almost always eat at yours, which isn't a bad thing, but a change would be nice. We could play games, maybe even do things with other couples."

"Other couples like who?" Neither of them knew many.

"Alexis and whoever she's dating." Which, at the time was, no one.

Zyair frowned. He liked Alexis and all, but she acted holier-than-thou, always talking about, "the Lord this, and the Lord that." Don't get him wrong, he believed in God and even attended church occasionally, but he just felt like she went overboard.

Besides, he didn't feel like hearing the *when-are-you-two-going-to-get-married* question. He was ready, but it seemed like Champagne wasn't. And he couldn't pressure her because when she was ready for marriage he wasn't.

"We can do all those things. But why don't we do something real wild and go to Hedonism?"

"Hedonism?" Champagne asked.

"Yep."

"Isn't that the all-nude resort?"

They had watched a special on it together. Zyair was ready to pack his clothes and go by the time the first commercial aired. He was afraid to say anything because he thought Champagne would ask him if he was crazy. His best friend Thomas went and said it was off the hook. People were fucking everywhere, and you could actually sit there and watch. Heck, some folks even let you join in. Now that he wasn't too sure about, but the watching part he could get with.

Champagne surprised him by saying, "It does sound interesting. Let me think about it."

"Are you serious? You're really going to think about it?"

"Yes, but we also need to work on doing some of the things I suggested as well."

The rest of the evening went without incident. Both of them felt a sense of relief about getting some things off their chest.

That night when they arrived home, Zyair made the effort to be romantic. While Champagne was in the shower, he dimmed the lights and tried to create a soft, seductive setting. He pulled out a bottle of wine, made a pallet of pillows near the fireplace and turned on some Luther. Then he went to join her.

Stepping into the bathroom, he asked, "Do you mind if I join you?"

Surprised, she told him, "Of course not." Actually she was about to get out but knew what he was trying to do and decided that, instead of pulling back, she would embrace this gesture.

A few seconds later, Zyair pulled back the doubled glass sliding door and took her in with his eyes. He loved what he saw.

Five years later, she was still beautiful, her skin flaw-less, smooth and tight, not an ounce of fat anywhere. How he could neglect her, he didn't know. His woman possessed what most men desired. Not only was she smart, sexy, beautiful, and compassionate, but she was also self-aware and selfless. She was also body and health conscious.

He roamed her body with his eyes and appreciated it once again. "I'm sorry I've been neglecting you. I'm going to start making it up to you from this day for-ward." He got undressed and stepped in the shower.

"The same here."

Champagne reached over with the washrag to rub his chiseled chest and washboard stomach. She teased him by moving her hands below his waist but stopped sud-denly and said, "Turn around. Let me wash your back."

"This isn't supposed to be about me. This is sup-posed to be about you." Zyair took the buffer and placed it to the side. He then took the lavender-scented body wash and placed his hands on her shoulders. "I love you, you know that, right?" He moved his hands from her shoulders to her breasts, letting the suds build up. "I can't imagine not being with you." He started massaging her nipples with the palms of his hands. "You're my future wife." He moved his hands down her stomach to her thighs, as the soap washed away, and got on his knees. "The mother of my children." He pushed her knees apart and Champagne leaned against the wall, the water still running.

Zyair palmed her pussy. "Do you want me to kiss you here or on your lips first?"

Champagne looked down, lust in her voice. "Those lips."

Zyair pulled her pussy lips apart and placed one of his fingers deep within her. "How's this?"

Champagne nodded.

"I don't understand that. Tell me, how's this?" He took his finger out and stuck his tongue deep inside her, causing her legs to give.

"What about this?" He took his tongue out and started playing with her clitoris, flicking it back and forth, then licking it.

Champagne grabbed his head and tried to pull it into her pussy. "I thought you forgot about that."

He looked up at her. "Let me do this my way. I don't want you to tell me that I just go for the gusto ever again."

"And I don't want to have to tell you that."

That night ended with a passion they both thought they wouldn't get back. Maybe this would be the new beginning they both desired.

CHAPTER THREE
"JUST GOT PAID"
JOHNNY KEMP

Champagne walked into her office, excited to start her day, only to find her boss, Charles Jackson, chilling in her space, behind her desk, like he belonged there. This irritated the hell out of her. She stopped in her tracks and started to curse his ass out but had to remind herself that his paying her was what paid her bills.

She loved her job. Maybe not where she worked and who she worked for, but she enjoyed doing what she did. She made people more famous than they already were. She came up with different ideas to do so, such as press conferences, dates with other stars, and magazine interviews. She also helped throw parties. Basically, she did what she had to do to get her clients more recognition.

In return she also received gifts, trips, and recognition, not to mention the friendships she developed with quite a few well-known actors, actresses, and singers.

Champagne started working for Jackson Publicity

seven years ago as an assistant, and had worked her way up to becoming one of the top publicists. She would have gotten there even sooner, had she slept with her boss, who'd tried on numerous occasions, only to have her turn him down. But, like a true trooper, he wouldn't give up.

"Champagne," Charles Jackson said.

"Jackson," Champagne replied. When she'd first started working there, she called him Mr. Jackson, but he kept insisting that she call him Charles, which was too personal for her liking, especially after his advances. Tired of the back-and-forth banter in regards to his name, she finally settled on calling him Jackson.

"Do you mind if I take my seat?" she asked in a tight tone that let him know she was annoyed.

"Oh, of course not." He stood up and moved from behind her desk, brushing up against her in the process.

She knew he did it on purpose and just wasn't feeling it today. Actually she was getting tired of it. Champagne looked at him with contempt. "So, what can I do for you?" She wanted him to get to the point of his visit and out of her sight. She knew there was a point, because he didn't come into her office often.

"Well, I'm getting you a partner."

Champagne looked at him. She knew if he was broke, no one would pay any attention to his short, yellow ass, but because he had money, it made him bearable, turning his five foot, seven inches into six feet. It always amazed her at how money could make a person more appealing.

"What?" She'd heard him but wanted him to repeat it. He knew she worked alone.

The other publicists had assistants and interns, but she didn't because she liked the flexibility of doing what she wanted, when she wanted, and not having to look over someone's shoulder or have them look over hers.

"I said, 'I'm getting you a partner.'"

"I've told you before, I don't want a partner."

"No, what you've said is that you don't want an assistant; there's a difference."

"I don't—" She was getting ready to say *understand*, but decided not to give him the satisfaction of seeing her upset.

"The person's name is Camille Ferguson, and she'll start in one week. On your desk is her resume and an outline of what I want you to show her."

"Fine. Whatever." Champagne knew in her gut that if she'd slept with him at the last conference they attended, this shit wouldn't be happening.

"Do you have a problem with my decision?" he taunted.

"Yes, Jackson, I do. I don't think I have to tell you that."

A month earlier, Champagne, Charles, and Tiffany Sweeps, one of the other women in the office, attended a Minority Business Conference in Washington, D.C., where they took a number of workshops and networked extensively. On the second night there, they joined a few other participants for drinks, and everyone got a little past tipsy.

Champagne knew this wasn't kosher and decided to head back to her hotel room to get some rest. She told the others that she would catch up with them tomorrow.

"I'll grab a taxi and head back with you," Jackson said. "It'll be my treat."

"Oh, no, you don't have to do that."

"I know I don't have to. I want to."

Champagne thought nothing of it and accepted.

In the car, only a few words were exchanged. When they arrived at the hotel, she said good night and started heading towards her room, only to find Jackson following behind her.

She turned around. "Are you following me?"

"Yeah. I was hoping we could stay the night together."

Jackson was less than a foot from her, and for the first time that night, she realized just how drunk he was. "I don't think so." She placed her key into the keyhole.

"Why not, Champagne? You know I want you and have been waiting for quite sometime." He was up in her face. "No one has to know. It'll be our little secret."

She knocked his hand down as he groped her breast. "I told you I'm not interested."

"Aw, come on." He leaned over and tried to kiss her. "Don't you know how far I can take you?"

She pushed him away. "You know this is sexual harassment, and you've been doing it for quite some time. I'd advise you to stop."

"Are you threatening me?"

"Do I have to?"

He took a step back. "Why are you so high and mighty? Just because you got a rich boyfriend don't mean shit. I've got almost as much money as he does."

"Please, just go away and leave me alone."

Jackson started walking away. "You know I can get pussy anytime. Don't think yours is special."

Champagne didn't feel a need to respond, she just shook her head, went into the room and avoided him for the rest of the conference. She spoke to him only if necessary.

When they returned to New York, the air was tight with tension, so she knew this was payback. It couldn't be anything else. She worked her ass off for him and got him the best clients possible. Even when he continued to be an asshole, she recruited for better clients and basically made his company the success it was today.

The time had come and Champagne knew what she had to do. It was time to move on. She'd been thinking about starting her own business anyway, and he'd just given her the opportunity.

She didn't want to react emotionally and up and quit in that moment. She had to sit down and plan her shit out. She wanted to take two clients with her, and she needed to prepare them.

Just knowing in that instant what her plans were calmed her down. She looked at Jackson and surprised him with, "Do what you have to do. If you think I need a partner, so be it. Now, if you don't mind, I have some phone calls I need to make."

Jackson was thrown off. He just knew she would be pissed. All the other women in the office kissed his ass, but not Champagne, not even after all these years. He figured he would have worn her down by now. He was in love with her, and was angry that the love wasn't being returned.

"I'm planning on having a staff meeting the end of this week before Camille starts, so check your schedule."

The second he left her office, Champagne was on the phone with Alexis. "Girl, are you busy for lunch? I need to talk."

"Never too busy for you."

"All right, let's meet at our spot in the village around one p.m."

"I'll be there."

For the rest of the morning, Champagne made phone calls, confirmed a few interviews, and started putting together a plan for her new venture.

What she had in mind was a dual public relations/personal assistant business that would cater to the wealthy, famous or not. If you could afford her services, she would take you on as a client. Her goal would be to make the client's life easier by arranging their schedules, setting up appointments, booking vacations. Basically managing their lives. Champagne knew this wasn't something she could do on her own and would definitely have to hire people.

Damn, I hope I'm not getting in over my head, she thought to herself.

Champagne and Alexis met at Bojo's, a vegetarian spot. Alexis didn't eat anything that lived and roamed the earth. This cracked Champagne up because she knew that Alexis grew up on ham and bacon.

As always, they sat outside. They loved to take in the sights and talk about the people that walked by. This day, they wouldn't be doing that. Champagne had some serious business at hand she needed to discuss.

"Would you like something to drink?" the waitress asked.

"Some water and the menu," Champagne replied.

"With lemon."

The waitress walked away.

"So, what's up, lady? What's new?"

"Beside the fact that I'm leaving my job?"

"Get out!"

"Girl, I can't do it anymore."

"What happened? Don't tell me Jackson came on to you again. I told you, you should have told Zyair a long time ago."

"And I told you, I had it under control. But that's not why. He had the audacity to tell me he hired a partner for me."

"A partner? Do you need a partner?"

"No, I don't need a damn partner. I know he's only doing this because I won't sleep with him."

"Well, sue his ass."

"I don't feel like going through all that. Plus, I have a better plan."

Alexis was all ears.

"I've brought him most of the top clients, and I'm going to take them with me when I leave."

"What about the contract you signed saying you couldn't do that?"

"Girl, I haven't signed a contract in over a year. I think it slipped his mind, because I've been there so long."

"You've got to do what's best for you."

Before Champagne could say anything else, the waitress placed their water on their table along with the menus.

Champagne waited until she walked away. "You know, me and Zyair had a talk."

"The talk?"

"Yeah, girl, the talk."

"It's about time. I was getting a little tired of you complaining to me about the same things over and over."

"I was not."

"Yeah, you were. You just didn't realize it. You were starting to sound like a broken record."

"Well, how come you didn't say anything?"

"Because I'm your friend, and that's what I'm here for, to listen."

* * *

Alexis and Champagne had been friends since childhood, going back as far as the fourth grade. They grew up in Neptune, a small town in New Jersey, and lived next door to one another.

Just as in any relationship or friendship, the two had been through their ups and downs. During their elementary, middle- and high-school years, you couldn't keep those two apart. They did everything together. They joined the same club, coordinated their clothes, calling each other the night before to find out what the other was wearing, and sometimes even liked the same boys. When that happened they both chose to leave it alone, because no man was gonna come between them.

Then there was the "thing" neither of them would ever discuss, playing house with one another. One would be the mommy, and the other, the daddy, and they would take turns kissing, rubbing up against each other, feeling each other's breast, and occasionally fingering each other. This went on mostly during the middle-school years, until they both became interested in boys. You would never think this took place, because they never acknowledged it.

They were different in personality and looks, total opposites, but both beautiful. Alexis was a yellow girl, as the boys called her, and shapely, so she usually received most of the attention. It never caused a problem because, unlike most light-skinned girls back in the day, she didn't flaunt it. She just wanted to be regular. It was already bad enough that she could barely walk down the street without some asshole yelling obscenities.

Not one to take any shit, she'd always speak up and tell someone what was on her mind, causing many fights in her youth. Things hadn't changed. As an adult, she still did this. The only change now was that she was saved, sanctified, and filled with the Holy Spirit.

Champagne felt like she went overboard with it, "The Lord this, the Lord that . . ."

It started when they went away to college in New York. Alexis met this guy called Brother. Yep, that was his real name. He wanted to be a minister and attended church regularly. When he and Alexis started dating, he invited her to church.

From that point forward, Champagne thought Alexis had joined a cult. She started being judgmental, quoting Bible verses. She'd stopped going out and drinking, acting like Champagne wasn't good enough. It was to the point that they stopped speaking for over a year.

One evening Champagne went out and was a little hungover with a headache. She went to Alexis's dorm, thinking she would find some comfort and support, only to have Alexis pray for her.

After listening to Alexis try to pray the demons out of her, she told her, "Listen, I love you and all, but I can't take you judging everything I do and say. So maybe we need to chill a little. If you really need me, I'm here for you but other than that, our friendship has reached a point where I no longer feel comfortable. I have to watch what I say and what I do. I'm always on guard and I feel like I can't be myself around you."

It was a heart-wrenching moment but something Champagne had to do for her peace of mind. It felt like a breakup. She cried for several days. She'd gotten used to picking up the phone and hearing her best friend's voice almost every day. Often she'd find herself picking up the phone, and dialing the number only to hang it back up. Homegirl was having withdrawal symptoms. She didn't realize how much she'd come to depend on Alexis.

It was Alexis who needed Champagne first. Brother broke her heart. She'd caught him cheating with one of the sisters in the church. At the time, Alexis still considered herself a virgin, as far as penetration. Orally, no.

She came crying to Champagne, "I thought he was perfect for me. He was saved, he went to church, he didn't pressure me to have sex."

I don't care how much church a man attends. Champagne thought. *If he's not getting the sex from his woman, he's getting the sex from somewhere.* But she didn't say anything, not wanting to kick a sister when she's down?

Alexis was still saved and she still had judgmental ways, but thank God, no longer went overboard with it. So when Champagne told her about she and Zyair going to Hedonism, Alexis didn't tell her she was going to hell, she just said, "Are you out of your mind?"

There was no way in the world she would take her man to a place filled with beautiful, naked women. She certainly didn't want to be around a bunch of naked men running around with their dicks hanging out. It just wasn't something she wanted to see and she couldn't understand why Champagne would either.

"Have you two lost your natural minds? I can't believe Zyair would even suggest such a thing. And for you to accept, what were you thinking?"

"I was thinking that it's time to add some spice into my relationship."

"That's the only plan you two could come up with?"

"You're judging, Alexis," Champagne told her in a tone that reminded her how far they'd come.

"I know, and I'm sorry. But there has to be some other way to add a spark to your relationship. Going to the freak beach? I don't know, girl. Something about it just ain't right. Plus, you ain't never walked around nobody naked, so how are you going to feel walking around strangers naked?"

"They won't know me, I won't know them—That's what's going to make it easy."

"You might be biting off more than you can chew. What are you going to do when his dick gets hard?"

"What do you mean, what am I going to do? Hop on it. Plus, there isn't too much he can do while I'm right there."

"Well, what are you going to do when you see some Mandingo-looking man and he turns you on?"

"What do you think I'm going to do? Stare with my tongue hanging out."

They shared a laugh, easing the tension that was forming. "You're sick, you know that?"

When Champagne returned to the office, she found a note on her desk from Jackson. He wanted her to put together a list of her clients and any pertinent information she wanted to share with Camille.

"To hell with that," Champagne said and packed up for the rest of the day.

CHAPTER FOUR
"BOYS"
MARY JANE GIRLS

Zyair was sitting in his office, a huge smile plastered on his face. He recalled the way Champagne surprised him by sucking his dick the night before. She did it like it was the best tasting dessert on this earth.

He'd arrived home from work late that night because of a party for an up-and-coming male fashion designer that wasn't scheduled to end until after one in the morning. Zyair was tired, and the only thing on his mind was climbing into the bed.

To his surprise, Champagne had other things in mind. "Hey, sweetie," she greeted him when he walked in. Looking sexy as hell, she was relaxed in the sitting room in a short black negligee and a glass of wine in her hands.

From an earlier conversation, he knew she'd had a rough day at work and was surprised to see her up. "Why aren't you in the bed?"

"I was waiting for you to come home."

"That's sweet, but you didn't have to do that."

"I know I didn't have to. I wanted to." Champagne

stood up and gave him a kiss, took his hand, and pulled him towards the bedroom. "Now go and take your shower, and I'll be out here waiting with a surprise."

Zyair questioned her with his eyes, but she wasn't giving anything away.

"Wash up good too," she told him. "Don't miss an inch."

While in the shower, Zyair wondered what she had planned. *She did say, "Don't miss an inch."* That meant a blowjob was in order, so he took extra care in cleaning his penis, under his balls, and his ass. One never knows.

Zyair stepped out the shower and into the bedroom. He dried himself off with the towel. On the nightstand next to the bed were some items. He took a closer look at them—Honey Dust Body Powder, Motion Lotion, and some weird-looking vibrator. "What the hell is that?" he asked.

"It's called a *cyberflicker*."

"And what is it suppose to flick. I know you don't plan on that going anywhere near me."

"Come here. Just relax and let me do my thing."

"I don't know."

"Trust me, I'm not going to do anything I'm sure you won't like."

Zyair sat on the bed cautiously.

Champagne straddled him and pushed him back.

"Don't you want to talk about your day?" he asked, playfully.

"No. I have something better in mind." Champagne kissed him on his eyelids, causing him to shut them and then traced his lips with her mouth. She pushed him back on the bed, moved her legs to rest between his, and placed her hands on his penis, massaging it.

Moving down his body with her tongue, she reached over for the Motion Lotion and ran her tongue over his shaft.

Zyair had his eyes open and watched her every move. She rubbed the lotion over his penis, and with each hand movement it was heating up.

Zyair moaned. "That feels good."

"Well, this is going to feel even better." Champagne blew on his penis, causing a heated sensation and then draped her mouth around it and circled it with her tongue, up to the head.

"Oh, girl, what are you doing?" Zyair tried to sit up, but she pushed him back down.

Instead of answering him, she proceeded to suck and lick every inch of him.

Zyair had his eyes closed and was giving his I'm-about-to-explode-at-any-moment face, when he heard this buzzing sound. "What the hell"—He opened his eyes in time to catch Champagne holding that "flicker thing" between his balls and ass. When she placed it there, his whole body tightened up.

"Come on, baby, relax. We said we wanted a change."

When he realized that she wasn't trying to put any-thing in him, he relaxed and enjoyed the feeling of the vibration, which ran up and down the length of his body. When she started licking his balls, he knew it would be over any minute.

"I'm going to come any minute now. Let me inside of you."

Champagne wasn't hearing it. She was enjoying the moment.

"Ugh!!!!!" Zyair yelled out. "I'm about to come."

Champagne replaced her mouth with her right

hand, dropped the flicker and massaged his balls with the left, while he exploded.

Afterwards Zyair looked at her with love. "That was the bomb." He didn't even question her about the new items. He'd just had the best orgasm in quite some time. If she'd only swallowed, that would have topped it off.

Champagne went to wash her hands and get a rag to wipe Zyair down. When she returned he was sound asleep. Smiling and wishing she could pat herself on the back, Champagne was pleased with herself.

So here Zyair sat, recalling last night and thinking to himself, I couldn't believe I let her put a damn vibrator anywhere near my ass.

Shaking his head, he tried to clear his thoughts and concentrate on the work that lay before him, but before he could even do that, there was knock at the door.

"Who is it?"

His employees knew not to bother him, especially if his door was closed. Every other Friday, he took care of the financial end of the business, paying bills, reviewing his cash flow and paying his employees, and this was one of those days. He did this religiously. It enabled him to know, on a consistent basis, what he was bringing in and what he was putting out. No one could or would ever try to cheat him out of a penny. He knew where every cent went.

His business allowed him the luxuries of his Cadillac, Jeep and Mercedes coupe that sat in the garage of his estate. It also allowed him to purchase Champagne the three-carat engagement ring she wore on her finger. Heck, it allowed him to be rich beyond his dreams and become richer in the upcoming years. Even his parents would be pleased at the success of the restaurant. Yes, it was a little more lavish than they'd initially planned, but to make money, you had to spend money. And he expanded on their dreams, bringing to fruition what they couldn't.

"It's Thomas, nig—" Thomas stopped short. He almost slipped up and said the whole word, but the last thing he needed to hear was Zyair chastising him, asking him why he had to be so hood, that there was a time and place for everything and his place of business wasn't it.

Thomas had heard the speech a thousand times and could repeat it word for word. "You can't come to my place of business acting like you're from the streets. My employees have to respect me and the way I am here with them is not the way I am with you," and on and on he'd go. Eventually, Thomas started to tune him out and would just nod his head as if he was listening.

"Hold up." Zyair got out of his chair and let Thomas in.

"What's up?" Thomas greeted.

They gave each other a pound.

"Nothing. Just taking care of business as usual."

"Want to go out for lunch?"

Zyair gave Thomas a long, steady look.

"What? Whacha lookin' at me like that for?"

"Today is the second Friday of the month. What do I do the second Friday of every month? My finances. You know this, and still you drop in and expect me to—"

Thomas stood up. "How about this? I have free

lunch while I'm here and we go out tonight instead, go a strip club, see some naked ass, have a couple of drinks. I'll call up Trevor and Wise and see if they want to join us."

Zyair really wasn't feeling it, but he knew he'd been neglecting his boys for the last month. He glanced at the calendar and recalled that it was Thomas's birthday. Not letting on that he forgot, he said, "Cool, anything for the birthday boy."

"Aww, nigga, I thought you forgot."

"You're my boy. I wouldn't forget your day."

"Yeah, okay. I saw you take a peek at the calendar."

Thomas and Zyair met during their first year of college. They attended Rutgers University in New Jersey together, and hung out with the same crowd. One evening when they were standing in the hall, Thomas overheard Zyair talking about his sloppy-ass roommate that was pledging a fraternity. "I'm about to go upside his head."

Thomas was going through the same thing with his roommate and was in the process of finding an apartment off campus. He'd need a roommate if he wanted extra cash to spend on the ladies. He decided to approach Zyair. "Yo, man, I'm about to get an apartment off campus, if we split the cost, we can get a two-bedroom and it'll save me a few dollars."

"Yeah, but what will it save me?" Zyair asked.

"I don't know what it'll save you, but you just might get peace of mind."

Zyair looked at him and tried to sum him up. He recalled seeing Thomas around campus talking to the finest ladies. He also knew that Thomas wasn't a slouch in the academics department. Although he dressed like a thug and talked liked he was from the streets, he ran track and stayed on the dean's list. He'd appreciate a change because his roommate was a slouch, loud, and irritating. Peace of mind was definitely something he could use.

"Yo, man, thanks. It sounds like a plan, but I need to see the place first." Zyair wasn't stupid. He knew that college students could only afford so much. He knew what he could afford, and he wasn't too sure if he wanted to give up safety for comfort.

The apartment turned out to be in a decent area of New Brunswick, close to downtown and near public transportation, so he moved in.

Thomas and Zyair got off to a smooth start. Both of them were neat freaks. Nothing was ever out of place. When they had women over, they were always impressed, especially when they learned they kept the place up themselves. They also never had any major disagreements, especially when it came to women. Zyair liked them attractive and smart, while Thomas liked them ugly and dumb. His theory was ugly women treat you better because they want to hold on to you and would do just about anything to make that happen. Zyair didn't have a theory. He just wanted someone he could carry a conversation and be seen in public with.

It wasn't long before they became the best of friends. They'd stay up late at night and talk about any and everything under the sun. They had each other's back. Where one might slack off in studies, the other picked up. They complemented one another, balanced each other out.

They became like brothers. Zyair's parents would send Thomas necessities when they sent Zyair's, who never felt cheated because he knew Thomas grew up in a foster home without family.

Thomas and Zyair still had each other's back. They'd

drink together and even go so far as to have sex in the same room. Well, that was before Champagne came along.

Occasionally Zyair would recall with disdain an incident that took place their senior year. They'd had a party to celebrate their upcoming graduation. Drinks were flowing, and weed was being passed back and forth like water. Everyone was having the time of their lives.

As the clock ticked and hours passed, the crowd started to disburse, until there was about ten people left. And what was a party with people dancing, laughing, and having a good time became an orgy.

How it happened is still beyond Zyair's knowledge. All he knew was that one minute he was kissing this girl on the couch, and two minutes later he looked up to find a group of five having sex near the fireplace, and two other couples off to the side doing their thing. Dicks were being sucked, people were fucking doggystyle.

There was no pussy eating. Back then, that was something the brothers denied doing, so to actually be seen doing it was out of the question.

Full of liquor and weed, Zyair decided to see just how far he could go with his female friend. It ended up being all the way.

Later that night, after everyone left, Zyair lay semiconscious out on his bed. He could barely move. His head was pounding. That night was his first night experimenting with weed, and he recalled hearing someone say it was laced with something.

Feeling a little out of it, he found himself falling asleep. He woke up with someone's lips wrapped around his penis. Not even bothering to open his eyes, he figured it was the girl he'd been with earlier. He decided to go with the flow and take the pleasure ride. He started moving his hips and grinding into the person's mouth and went to reach for their head when he heard his door open.

"What the fuck?" Thomas yelled out.

Zyair opened his eyes and looked down to find Ty'ron, a classmate and fellow partygoer with his dick in his mouth. Shocked, embarrassed, and confused because it was feeling so good, Zyair's initial reaction was to jump up and push Ty'ron's head away. He then kicked him in the chest, causing him to fall back. Zyair was about to beat his ass to pulp, but Ty'ron got up to run out the room.

"Close the door!" Zyair called out.

Thomas did as he was told.

Zyair looked at Thomas and tried to convince him. "Yo, man, I'm not gay. I was in here passed out. I wake up and this motherfucka has my dick in his mouth." Zyair took a step towards Ty'ron.

Ty'ron covered his face, like the punk he was, and immediately started apologizing.

Zyair was up on him when Thomas said, "Wait! Wait!" and stood between them.

"Move out of my way, man, or you're going to get hurt too."

"Nah, man. I've got a better idea. Let's humiliate him instead. That's what we used to do in foster care."

"Fuck humiliation! He needs his ass kicked!"

Thomas started to unzip his pants and turned towards a frightened Ty'ron. "You want to suck some dick? Here's a dick for you?"

Zyair was shocked. "Yo, man, what the fuck are you doing?"

"Let him finish his job on the both of us."

Zyair looked at Thomas like he'd lost his mind. "I ain't gay, man."

"And neither am I. He started it, let him finish."

Zyair, not being sure what to do and caught between confusion and anger, decided to just follow Thomas's lead, and together they forced Ty'ron to do them both. They knew he wouldn't say anything for fear of what it would do to his reputation.

This incident stayed their secret. They never told a soul about it and discussed it only once, and that was the following day.

"Yo, man, what made you come into my room?" Zyair asked.

"Well, when you were doing Sarah, I saw Ty'ron watching, and it looked like he was watching you harder than her. When you went to your room, he said he was going to the bathroom. Something just didn't feel right. He was taking a long-ass time to come back, so I thought I'd check on you. Shit, you better be glad I did because ain't no telling how far he would have tried to go."

"How come you just didn't let me beat his ass?"

"That would have been too easy."

"I don't know, Thomas. I don't feel right about what we did. I'm not gay, and the shit feels wrong."

"Man, please . . . just because you let another man suck your dick don't make you gay. When I was in foster care, it was either that or get beat down. Which route would you have taken? Don't even worry about it. It's between us. We don't even have to talk about it anymore."

To Zyair, just because it wasn't talked about didn't mean it didn't happen. It was something he thought about occasionally but never discussed ever again with anyone. He decided that the incident was something he would take to his grave.

Later that evening Zyair and Champagne sat on the couch discussing Champagne's business plan. Suddenly Zyair glanced at his watch. "Oh shit."

"What's up?" Champagne asked.

"I forgot I told Thomas and the boys I'd hang out with them. Today is Thomas's birthday."

Champagne didn't know whether to believe him or not. It's funny how insecurity can creep up on you at any given moment. Ever since they'd had their we-need-a-change-in-our-relationship talk, she'd been second-guessing herself. Then out of the clear blue sky, Zyair informed her that he was hanging out that night, which didn't make it any better. She knew that he was anal about his schedule.

"Where are y'all going?" she asked.

"I'm not sure, but I'll call you while I'm out."

That made her feel a little better, because he couldn't be doing too much if he telephoned her.

"What time do you think you'll be back?"

Zyair stood up. "Why the third degree?"

"What? I can't ask you any questions?"

Not in the mood for an argument, Zyair chose not to answer. Instead, he just leaned over and kissed her on the forehead. "I'll call you while I'm out."

CHAPTER FIVE
"FRIENDS"
WHODINI

Zyair and his boys had taken to doing something at least once a week.

While in the mall shopping, Champagne admitted to Alexis that she was a little jealous. Shopping was something Champagne hated to do. She'd rather order out of a catalog or off the internet. Mall shopping just didn't do it for her, with people everywhere, clothes picked all over, and salespeople in your face. "Can I help you, Can I help you?"

She knew it was their job, but sometimes she just wanted to yell, "Go away."

"Girl, please . . . don't be jealous. A man needs his space, just like a woman does. I'm sure you don't want to be cooped up under some man all day every day. You need to be you and let him be him."

"I know, but I've gotten spoiled. It's just been me and him for the past couple of months."

"Reality check! You've also been miserable. Plus, you're going to have him for the rest of your life. What's a couple of hours here and there?"

* * *

Champagne knew Alexis was right. She also knew she was going through some emotional shit right now. She felt like she was on some sort of roller-coaster. She was definitely leaving her job. She was going to start a new company, and to top all that off, Jackson expected her to train the new girl. She was feeling a little sensitive and a lot overwhelmed.

Camille, her new partner came in making demands, acting like she was Whitney or some other diva. Champagne knew that Camille and Jackson were fucking. The way he was rolling out the red carpet for her, there couldn't have been any other reason. He was even paying her a higher starting salary than normal, and as if that weren't enough, what really broke the camel's back was when he tried to hand over one of Champagne's better clients, who politely told him that the only person he was interested in working with was Champagne.

Thank God, she had already talked to some of her clients and informed them she was leaving. Most of them said they would like to continue having her service them, no matter where she was employed. She informed them that she would have to look over their contracts first. She didn't want to get into trouble legally by stealing clients under contract. If she discovered she couldn't be held liable for them leaving, so be it.

"You know, tomorrow is the day I'm officially handing in my resignation."

Alexis didn't' hear her because she was looking at a pair of shoes. Champagne knew not to repeat herself because nothing came between Alexis and her shoes.

"What do you think of these?" Alexis held up a pair of white three-inch heels.

"I don't like white shoes, you know that."

"Well, humor me."

"Anyway, I'm resigning tomorrow, and I'm a little nervous about it."

"That's understandable." Alexis looked at the cashier and told her she'll take the shoes in a size eight. "Champagne, honey, you're about to embark on a big project. Starting your own business isn't something small. You have a right to be nervous. I believe in you, though. You're smart, and you're a go-getter. It'll all work out."

Champagne heard what Alexis was saying. She knew she was right about her being a go-getter. Shit, mostly everything in life she wanted to achieve she'd achieved. She and her brother Sir were raised by a single mom, who tried her damnedest to instill in them a sense of pride and self-esteem. She told them over and over that they could be whatever they wanted to be and do whatever they set their minds on doing. Champagne believed her. Sir didn't. Growing up, neither of them knew their fathers.

Sir was two years older than Champagne and always seemed to have a hard time, as a child and as a man. It was like he was cursed. He just couldn't seem to get it together. He did average in high school, flunked out of college, couldn't find a job and turned to drugs.

Champagne blamed it on the fact that there wasn't a male figure around, someone to guide him and be an example. Champagne and her mother tried to help him the best they knew how, but to no avail. Sir committed suicide at the age of twenty-two. It devastated Champagne. She went into a shell for over a year, not talking to anyone or doing anything. School was all that mattered to her. She was determined to graduate at the top of her class.

Champagne became an overachiever and sometimes she still found herself falling into the am-I-doing-enough, am-I-achieving-enough trap. Every time you turned around there was something else she wanted to do. First, she wanted to be a teacher, then a counselor, then in the arts. She went back to school to get her master's and was considering going back to get her doctorate. Why? Because she could. She often wondered, *Why settle, when the world has so much to offer?*

What drove her were memories of her brother and his unhappiness, his insecurities, his failures and, most of all, his suicide. There was no way she would be so displeased with her life that she would take her own, so her response was to consume herself with work and Zyair. She knew it was unhealthy, but she didn't know what else to do about it.

After her brother's death, she and her mother barely spoke. Whenever she tried to initiate a relationship, she was pushed away. Eventually she gave up, but her plan was to correct that soon.

"You know what? You're right, I can do this. I'm intelligent, I'm talented, I've made some of the clients more popular than they ever believed possible. Most of them want to come with me when I leave, so what do I have to be concerned about?"

Alexis smiled. "Now that's what I like to hear."

"What's on your agenda this evening?" Champagne

didn't have anything planned, Zyair was working late, and she didn't feel like being by herself.

"I've got a hot date, girl."

"Get the hell out of here. When was the last time you've been on a date? Does he go to your church or something?"

"No, he don't go to my church. And why you gotta rub in the fact that I haven't been on a date in some time? Actually I met him at the Laundromat."

"The Laundromat? What were you doing at the Laundromat? You have a washer and dryer at home."

"Something is wrong with the dryer. Anyway, let me finish. I had just finished putting my clothes in the dryer and was about to walk out when this fine, with a capital *F*, brother strutted in. I was about to leave, but I hesitated."

"You hesitated?" This surprised Champagne because Alexis never ever made the first move. She was a Christian and believed that women shouldn't go looking for men, that men are the hunters.

"Yeah, girl, that's how fine he was. Not only that, but there was this magnetism about him that just drew me in."

Champagne couldn't believe what she was hearing. She laughed. "Magnetism?"

Ignoring her, Alexis continued, "So I turned around and decided to wait until my clothes dried and see if he would strike up a conversation."

"Did he?"

"After a good ten minutes of waiting and not even a hello, I said to him, 'Are you new around here? I've never seen you before.'"

"No, you didn't."

"Yes, I did, girl. It was a weak line, but it worked.

He's new in town. Only been here for three weeks. His name is Khalil. He works construction."

That surprised Champagne because Alexis usually didn't go for blue-collar brothers. "Construction?"

"Yes, construction. Anyway, we talked a little more, and he asked me if I'd like to go out for dinner one night. So I said yes."

"You said yes?"

"I figure why not. I've been praying for God to send me the right mate, and I'm not saying he's it, but I know I need to be more open and stop carrying this list in my head on what the perfect man is."

"I know that's right, because your list was unrealistic."

Champagne recalled Alexis and her pulling out a piece of paper with "the qualities of a good man" on it. It went something like this: Christian man, honest, hard-working, making 60G a year, over six feet tall, in good physical condition, great lover, no kids, must be at least thirty.

After reading the list, Champagne told her, "I've already got the man."

"Don't brag."

"What are you willing to compromise on?" Champagne asked.

"Well, you know there's one thing I'm not comprising on, and that's him being a Christian."

"Is he?"

"Yes. I asked him what churches have he attended since he's been in town. He said that was the first thing he did, find some place to serve the Lord."

"Get out of here."

"I know, right. "

Champagne was glad for Alexis and told her so. "Make sure you call me, no matter what time it is, and let me know how things go."

"You know I will."

They shopped a little while longer and separated in the parking lot.

Champagne hoped this Khalil guy was the one for Alexis. She was tired of seeing her best friend single, and thought she deserved a man, some children, and the white picket fence with the big yard, all the things little girls dream of having when they picture their lives as women.

When Champagne was young she dreamed of being rich beyond her means, jet-setting from place to place, purchasing whatever she wanted, whenever she wanted it. A man was never in the picture. Don't get it twisted, Champagne didn't think she'd be lonely for life, but her main concern was to make her life successful. She'd been in and out of relationships, mostly short-term, dated occasionally, and had sex once in a while. Then she met Zyair and her life plan changed.

One evening Champagne and Zyair were out to dinner. Their relationship was just getting off the ground, and they were both in denial of their feelings toward each other. Of course, neither wanted to be the first to admit that they were falling in love. They were both afraid of jumping into a relationship headfirst, due to past romantic failures. They both tried to be nonchalant about what they had, not labeling it and just letting it be, although, neither could deny their feelings were growing stronger by the day.

While at dinner, Zyair asked, "What does a man represent to you?"

Thrown off, Champagne asked, "What kind of question is that?"

"Just a question." Zyair wanted to see where her head was. He was ready to make her "the one."

"I don't know how to answer that."

"Answer it honestly."

Shit, that was a question she'd never given any real thought to. She knew what a man was supposed to represent, security, peace, family, a sense of well-being, but up to this point she hadn't seen any evidence of that. To her, a man just represented companionship, a date, and sex. She didn't want to tell him that because thinking it made her feel a little apprehensive, so saying it out loud surely wouldn't be any better.

"Companionship," she told him, leaving the rest out.

He was satisfied. "What's *companion*, to you?"

"Someone to talk to, someone to share your wishes, your dreams, and your securities with. Someone to cuddle with and make love to."

Zyair knew he could be those things.

Returning to the present moment, Champagne glanced at her Gucci watch, an extravagant gift from Zyair, and saw that time was ticking. Sometimes she felt like he spent way too much money on her. Not that she was complaining, because being spoiled was nice, she just wasn't used to it. She made well over 70K a year and saved more than she spent, which was a good thing now that she thought about it, especially since it allowed her to start her own business.

Instead of going home, Champagne decided to go to the office to copy the clients' files she was interested in taking with her. She'd been glancing through them all week but, not wanting to make it too obvious, decided to wait until the last possible moment to make copies.

No one should be in the office other than the security guard, who she knew wouldn't say a word, because Jackson treated him with arrogance and disregard.

When Champagne arrived at the office she was surprised that Jimmy, the security guard, wasn't at his post. As she walked towards her office, she noticed that Jackson's door was slightly ajar and that a ray of light was shining through the crack. She could also hear soft music playing in the background.

Knowing she was wrong and nosy for what she was about to do, she moved closer to the door and peeked through the crack, only to see Camille dancing seductively in front of Jackson. The form-fitting skirt and jacket she wore to the office was on the floor, while she paraded in a red spaghetti-thin G-string panty, black thigh-highs, and a red lacy bra with her breast flowing over the top.

Champagne looked at Camille and noticed that she appeared much thicker in the near-nude than fully dressed. It was a kind of thickness that would turn on any man, or woman if you went that way. It was definitely turning on Jackson, whose attention was razor-sharp, watching every hip thrust and every pelvic movement.

When Camille's hand caressed her stomach and moved on to her breast, squeezing her nipples, his eyes followed. When her hands moved down between her legs, rubbing her pussy, his eyes followed. Champagne found her eyes following as well.

When Camille turned around, Champagne noticed that her eyes were closed. She bent over in front of Jackson, and he grabbed her ass and started massaging her buttocks. Champagne could feel her pussy walls opening and closing, and that could only mean one thing. The scene before her was turning her on. She didn't quite know how to react to this. On one hand she was disgusted with herself. On the other, she had to admit that curiosity was getting the better of her.

Common sense finally took over, and she turned away and hurried towards her office. Sitting behind her desk, she tried to catch her breath. There was no way she was going to stay here and make copies, after the episode she'd just witnessed.

Now, the challenge was getting out unnoticed and unheard. Grabbing the files she wanted from inside her desk, she walked softly into the hallway, careful not to make a sound. She made it down the hallway, past Jackson's office, and out the front door. Everything in her wanted to turn around and take one last look, but the fear of being caught was enough to make her leave the premises.

On the way home, Champagne stopped off at Kinko's to make the copies she needed. She knew Zyair wouldn't be home until late that night. There was a conference being held at his restaurant, and he liked to stay and make sure things ran at a smooth pace.

Pulling up into the driveway, Champagne had a brief flashback of Jackson and Camille. She shook the image out of her head, but not before recalling the fullness of Camille's breasts. "What the hell is wrong with me?" she asked herself.

CHAPTER SIX
"CAUGHT IN THE MIDDLE"
WILL SMITH

Zyair was looking across the floor at a group of people gathered near the bar and couldn't help but notice that one of the men in the group looked real familiar. At least, his profile did, because he hadn't yet turned around to give Zyair a full view of his face. Taking a step forward to get a closer look, Zyair turned quickly because, at that exact moment, the brother turned around. It was the last person on earth Zyair wanted to see, Ty'ron the dicksucker. It was a college memory Zyair wanted to erase from his mind altogether.

Ty'ron noticed Zyair the second he walked in the restaurant and was torn between leaving and staying. But leaving really wasn't an option, since he was one of the speakers. The conference was for Financial Advisors, and Ty'ron worked for one of the top Black-owned companies in the United States. With the knowledge that he possessed, he was capable of making someone rich beyond their dreams.

When Ty'ron first entered the restaurant and saw

Zyair, he didn't know whether to approach him and apologize, or knock the shit out of him. The college incident stayed in the back of his mind. He knew he was wrong for violating Zyair in his sleep. In a way he felt that he deserved what Zyair and his boy Thomas did, but then again, he would have preferred the ass-whupping Zyair was going to lay on him.

Ty'ron couldn't help but wonder if he and Thomas were still in touch. *Damn, Zyair still looked good as hell. He was always a handsome man. If given the chance I'd turn his ass out.* Ty'ron knew he was dead wrong for these thoughts. Instead of focusing on Zyair, he needed to focus on his speech.

In the meantime, Zyair glanced at Ty'ron and wondered if he was gay. He had to be, the way he'd sucked his dick like a pro. From his appearance, you couldn't tell because he looked all man. In this day and age you could never tell a person's sexuality by their appearance. All you had to go on was their word.

Turning around, Zyair decided it was time to leave. All of a sudden he felt a headache coming on and was developing an upset stomach. Finding his hostess DaNeen, Zyair told her, "I'm leaving you in charge."

"You are?" DaNeen asked, surprised.

Zyair normally stayed to the end when something was going on in the restaurant. "Yes. Just make sure everything is cleaned and locked up."

"I will. You don't have to worry about a thing."

"All right, I'll see you tomorrow." On that note, Zyair walked out.

Once in the car Zyair pounded on the steering wheel. He yelled out loud, "Shit!" He'd put the incident so far in the back of his mind, and to have it standing there, staring into his face, was mind-blowing. Now was definitely the time for that vacation he and Champagne had discussed.

Which is just what Champagne suggested the second Zyair walked in. She didn't let him get in the door good. "Baby, let's take that vacation we talked about as soon as possible."

"Whoa, whoa. Where did this come from?"

"I'm just ready to go. Tomorrow is my resignation day, and before I start a new venture I'd like to spend some time with you," she said, following him into the living room.

"I hear you. Shit, I'm ready for that vacation just as much as you are. Where do you want to go?"

"I thought we discussed Hedonism?"

This surprised Zyair. When he'd first suggested it, he didn't think she'd agree. "For real?"

"Yes, for real." Champagne was half-amused hearing the excitement in his tone. She also knew that his imagination was running wild and after witnessing Jackson and Camille, she knew she could do the voyeur thing. "Let's call the travel agency and leave this weekend."

Zyair almost said that was to soon that he needed to arrange things at the restaurant. Normally he'd make sure sure things were in order, doubled check the calendar, speak with his employees and give them a "watch everything and make sure nothing goes awry" speech. This time he wasn't going to do that. He knew it was time to trust them, to let go and enjoy life a little more.

Plus, after seeing Ty'ron, he needed the vacation just as much as Champagne and the sooner the better, the farther away the better. "Let's do it." Zyair said.

Pleased, Champagne kissed him on the cheek and suggested they go swimming.

"I don't feel up to it."

"But I have a surprise for you." Champagne was using her suggestive tone.

Zyair recognized it, but the headache that started earlier was now pounding. He took her hand. "I'm sure you do, sweetie, but I have a terrible headache. I need to take some Advil and lay down."

Disappointed because her plan was to put it on him, Champagne said, "Oh, okay." She kissed him on the cheek and told him to get comfortable while she made him some chamomile tea to relax him.

The following day Champagne was standing in Jackson's office. Her heart was racing. Uncertain about how he would respond, she was anxiety-ridden and fearful. "I'm resigning," she told him. "I'm giving you one month's notice, but I'm leaving for a one-week vacation, so I won't be in next week and—"

"Whoa, whoa, hold up. Hold the fuck up. What the fuck are you talking about? What's this all about?"

Champagne was fed up, she was done, and no longer had to put with his attitude, and she wanted him to know it. "I know you need to stop talking to me like that."

Going on, Jackson said, "Do you really think you could just come in here and quit just like that? Like you haven't signed a contract? Like you're not obligated to several clients? And on top of everything else, you tell me, not ask me, but tell me you're taking a one-week vacation."

"I'm not a child, Jackson. I'm not a child, and I'm not one of your bitches that need to ask your permission. As a matter of fact, I'm a grown-ass woman that hasn't signed a contract in over two years. Your ass forgot, and I didn't mention it. This is your business. That's the kind of shit *you*'re supposed to keep tabs on, not me. I'm going on vacation. I have more than enough time saved up, and I've contacted my main clients and told them I was resigning. I also informed them that your lover, Camille, would be taking over." That part slipped out, but Champagne was on a roll. "Not only that, but—"

"But nothing, but nothing. You owe me. I made you!" Jackson said hysterically. He depended on Champagne more than he thought. She'd trained everyone that came in after her and made him tons of money. She'd convinced his best clients to stay with him when he acted like an asshole, and was always the middleman when there was conflict.

What the hell did she mean, she hasn't signed a contract in two years. Thinking about it, he realized she was right. She hadn't, and that possibly meant that some of the clients hadn't either. This wasn't something he felt like dealing with. Jackson knew that the right thing to do would be to sweet-talk her, offer her a raise, maybe even a partnership, but his anger got the better of him. "You know what? You can leave right now. I don't need any notice. Pack your shit and go."

Champagne looked him up and down and shook her head. "That's just what I wanted to hear." Then she turned around and strolled out of his office, leaving him with a stunned look on his face.

"She'll be back," Jackson said from the behind the door, trying to convince himself.

When Champagne stepped into the hallway, some of the employees were smiling at her. They'd overheard the exchange and gave her the thumbs-up. Most of them wanted to quit as well but just didn't have the heart to.

"You're doing the right thing," Takia, Jackson's secretary, told her. "I might be right behind you."

Smiling, Champagne decided to give her a life lesson, "Takia, you're a quick learner. You're smart and intelligent. Life has so much to offer, yet you take the abuse from Jackson on a daily basis. I know he pays you well, but you have to value yourself a little more, know your worth and—"

Jackson walked out of his office and glared at her. "I thought you were leaving?"

Champagne looked at him and rolled her eyes. She started walking away and felt proud of herself. She was on her way to bigger and better things, things she'd worked hard for and thoroughly deserved.

CHAPTER SEVEN
"FREAKS COME OUT AT NIGHT"
WHODINI

The flight to Jamaica went smooth. That's the way it ought to be when you're traveling first-class. Champagne read a book, while Zyair napped. Zyair's napping came as a big surprise because he had a slight case of claustrophobia, and when in flight was always filled with nervous energy. So to see him resting and at peace was a good sign to Champagne.

When they finally landed, Champagne glanced around in awe as she always did whenever they traveled, each new place providing a new adventure, a different thrill. She loved traveling and seeing new cultures. She'd take in the sights, the sounds, the aromas, and the people.

Glancing around, she noticed that the majority of tourists were white. It always amazed her how white people would travel thousands of miles to be surrounded by Black people.

Champagne recalled a rerun of the Essence Awards when Mos Def, the rapper/poet/actor, made the comment that he loved his people because they were his.

She couldn't agree more. She knew and understood just what he was saying. She loved the cadence of Black speech, the pimp walk, the sultry walk, and the various skin tones of her people. She couldn't imagine wanting to be anything other than Black.

She and Zyair saw a group of women singing, "Welcome to Jamaica," and they stopped to listen for a brief moment.

"Come on, baby, we don't want to miss the shuttle." Zyair pulled her along, past a group of young boys asking in a low tone if they wanted to purchase some ganja.

"No, thanks," Zyair quickly replied.

Together Champagne and Zyair carried with them four suitcases. They were seated on the shuttle bus, next to a white couple tonguing one another down. They looked at one another, kissed quickly and held hands, each attempting to prepare themselves for the all the stories they'd heard about Hedonism.

The white man came up for air and looked at Zyair. "What resort are you going to?"

"Hedonism."

Glancing down at their bags, the couple smiled and said, "First time, huh?"

"Is it that obvious?" Champagne asked.

The couple laughed.

"Believe me," the man said, "you won't be needing all that luggage." Then he introduced himself as Joe, and his wife as Cassandra.

"I'm Zyair, and this is my wife, Champagne."

"What unusual yet beautiful names," Cassandra told them.

Champagne wondered if she was seeing things. *Did she just wink at me?*

"This is our third time visiting," Cassandra said.

"Wow, you must like a lot," Champagne slumped back into is bed.

"You have no idea," Joe said.

"Is it everything they say, sexy, full of surprises, naked people everywhere, people having sex out in the open?"

"Yep. You definitely have to be open-minded."

Neither Champagne nor Zyair said anything because they thought they were open-minded, but were they really? Would they be able to handle all the naked-ness?

As they drove through the streets of Jamaica, the sun was beaming in their faces and Champagne pulled out her shades, put them on, and glanced at the couple that sat beside them. *Freaks*? she wondered.

Zyair wondered if they were swingers, and after looking and listening he knew they were.

"How long before we get there?" Zyair asked the driver.

"About an hour and a half," he replied.

Champagne glanced at her watch and sighed. They'd only been in the van for fifteen minutes, and it seemed like an hour. She was hungry, tired, thirsty, and in need of a stretch. Along with all that, she was a little disap-pointed at the sights. She had pictured Jamaica as an exotic-looking island, plush land, greenery everywhere. She'd pictured the people dressed in rich-textured cloth-ing, walking around like kings and queens. She'd pic-tured the whole island looking like a resort and thought the homes would look like castles, but what she saw was far from what she imagined. Instead, there were ghettos and poverty everywhere, kids running around with no shoes on, their bodies covered in dirt and dusty clothes, and many were selling various items on the side of the street. Young and old were begging. It was heartwrenching.

Champagne was ready to get out the van, stretch her legs, breathe, and make sure she was alive. First of all, the driver was speeding along with all the other drivers. In Jamaica they drove on the opposite side of the street, and every couple of miles, there was a sign that would read: Over 200 people killed on these roads, drive carefully.

After about the fifth sign, she tapped Zyair on his shoulder and asked him, "Do you see those signs? Can you believe it?"

The driver, overhearing this, said, "Don't worry, pretty lady. I take good care of you, make sure you get there safe."

Champagne smiled in response. She loved his strong, confident accent.

"Do you think we can stop and get something to drink?" Cassandra asked.

Everyone was in agreement.

"Sure," the driver replied. "There's a little spot coming up. We'll stop there, get food, drinks, and eat some conch."

"Conch?" Zyair asked. "What's that?"

"It's what the natives eat, especially the men. Makes them strong, virile, at attention."

Everyone laughed because they knew what he meant when he said *at attention*.

"I eat it every day, and I have six kids."

No one said a word. The last thing either couple wanted was six kids.

A few minutes later, they were pulling up in front of something that looked like a shack on the outside but was a full-fledged dining area on the inside. The ladies sat, while the men went to order their food.

While the men were away, Champagne wanted to

hear more about Hedonism, so she asked Cassandra, "Do the people really have sex out in the open?"

"Yeah, girl, you see the more people drink and the later it gets, the more their inhibitions are down. What side are you and your husband staying on?"

"What do you mean what side?"

"The nude, prude, or optional side."

Champagne laughed. "You mean to tell me that's how they separate the people?"

"Yes, that way no one is insulted or offended, and they don't have to take part in something they don't feel comfortable with."

Before she could go on, Zyair and Joe appeared with platters of the spiciest aromatic foods.

Champagne could feel her mouth watering. "Where's our driver?" she asked, looking around.

Zyair nodded in the direction the driver was in. "Out back smoking weed with the owner."

"I don't know if I feel comfortable riding on these dangerous roads with someone that's getting high."

"They do this every day here," Joe informed her. "Don't worry about it. It's a part of their lifestyle, their culture. To them marijuana is a cigarette."

Zyair sat across from Champagne. "Joe was telling me to be aware of the people who try to befriend us in Hedonism."

Champagne addressed Joe and wondered if it's him and his wife they should be aware of. "Really? Why?"

"Well, first of all, you two are a very attractive couple, and that's make you swinger material."

"Swinger material?" There was no way in hell Champagne would be swinging with or from anything other than her man's dick.

"A lot of that goes down here. As a matter of fact,

that's why a lot of people vacation here, to do things they normally wouldn't do."

"So what you're saying is people just approach you and be like, 'Let's fuck'?" Zyair asked.

"What they normally do is send the woman over. She'll try to befriend Champagne and maybe invite you out to dinner and for drinks."

Cassandra picked up from there. "Then she'll ask you if you want to dance, and that's when she'll make her move and try to test the waters, see how close she can get to you, feel you up. She'll say suggestive things, and the next thing you know, everybody is doing the wild thing."

Zyair was liking what he was hearing. Just the thought of another woman feeling Champagne up and she letting it happen was getting his dick hard. But her being with another man was a definite no-no. He wasn't trying to hear that.

"Oh hell no!" Champagne declared, "I'm not with any of that."

Cassandra laughed. "Never say never, girl."

Just from her saying that, Champagne and Zyair knew they were with "the freakism."

Back in the van, after eating and having a couple of drinks, everyone fell asleep, but not before Zyair whispered in Champagne's ear, "I can't wait to make love to you on the beach."

As they got closer to the resort, everyone took notice of the tight security at the gated resort. It was like being in a different world. One second they were in the ghetto, the next, in paradise.

They climbed out of the van, and someone came to grab their bags.

Champagne and Cassandra hugged, and Zyair and Joe shook hands.

"We'll see you around," Joe said as he and Cassandra walked away. "Maybe we can hook up later for drinks or something."

"That'll be cool," Zyair replied. There was no doubt about it. They were going to be on the nude side.

Zyair and Champagne found out they were on the optional side. As they were led to their rooms, many of the workers greeted them, telling them, "Enjoy your stay."

"Wow! Everyone is so nice and courteous here," Champagne commented.

"They have to be, if they expect everyone to be ass out."

Together they laughed and entered the room.

"There's no TV." Zyair walked over to pull back the curtains and was caught off guard when he saw a dick swinging left and right and breasts bouncing. "Oh shit!" he yelled out.

Champagne walked over to see what caused the alarm.

"You think we can do it?" Zyair asked.

"After a whole bottle of something."

Together they stood and continued looking out the window for a full five minutes.

"You tired?" Zyair asked.

"I'm too excited to be tired. Let's take a quick shower and walk around, see what this place has to offer."

They found out that it had a lot to offer, and it only took the first night. They met up with Joe and Cassandra, who were sitting with a group of people at the bar, where the women were topless and the men had towels around their waist.

Zyair and Champagne felt a little ill at ease, but got over it after a few drinks. Champagne wore booty shorts and a skimpy top, something she would never wear out in the open in the States, and Zyair wore swimming trunks. There was no way he was showing his shit.

Everyone was a little tipsy, and someone suggested they go over to the Jacuzzi. Champagne looked over at Zyair, who was drinking more than usual.

"I'm with it, if you are," he said.

So over to the Jacuzzi they went. There was nakedness everywhere. Zyair looked at Champagne to see if she was uncomfortable. He whispered, "It's up to you."

"I don't know." Champagne wasn't sure how she felt about Zyair being around all these naked women and wondered if Zyair was comparing dick sizes.

"Aw, come on, don't be scared," someone yelled out. "It's nothing. No one even cares. Look around you."

They did, and no one did care. People were just walking about, drinking, playing volleyball, all naked, like it was the most natural thing in the world.

"You know what? Fuck it. We're in another part of the world, we don't know anyone here, so why not?" Led by the liquor, Champagne slipped out of her shorts.

Zyair noticed she didn't have any panties on.

She then took her top off and climbed into the Jacuzzi. Everyone started clapping.

A surprised Zyair followed her lead. While in the Jacuzzi, Zyair tried to take in the sights without making it too obvious.

Champagne caught on and told him, "It's okay. You can look."

The couple right next to them started kissing. There was nothing wrong with it. It just caught them off guard, but it became something when the woman straddled the man and rode him right in front of everyone.

Feeling more than a slight uneasiness, neither Zyair

nor Champagne knew how to react. Do they watch? Do they turn away? Do they say something? They decided to do what everyone was doing—Ignore it, and act nonchalant, laid back, and indifferent, as if it didn't matter one way or the other.

They continued to drink and chat with a couple across from them. That didn't last too much longer because, right in the middle of their discussion, the man sat up on the edge of the Jacuzzi and his mate started sucking his dick.

Unable to control himself, Zyair told Champagne, "I'm ready to go to our room."

She couldn't agree more. Standing up and feeling overexposed once again, this time nipple protruding and sexual energy racing through her body, she started to climb over the edge.

Zyair pulled her down. "I need a few seconds."

She took that to mean, *His dick is hard and he doesn't want everyone to see.*

After a brief moment, they climbed out the Jacuzzi and somehow made it to their room without attacking one another.

They never made it to the bed, though, because when they stepped through the door, Champagne told Zyair, "Fuck me." She'd been wanting to tell him that as soon as she saw that lady straddle her man.

Champagne let out a low and deep moan. She was close to an orgasm, a sensation she'd been wanting. Zyair didn't know that she had already began playing with her pussy under the pressure of the water, so when he said he was ready to go, she was with it.

Taking his hand and leading him over to the dresser closest to the door, she leaned over, and took her fingers and spread her pussy wide open from behind.

Savoring the moment, Zyair stood with a gleam in

his eyes. Loving her aggressiveness, he stepped closer, grabbed her ass cheeks, and entered her with force.

"Shit!" Champagne cried out. She wasn't expecting that. She thought he would try to tease her, but she enjoyed this just the same.

Slowly leaving the walls of her wetness, he pulled back and entered her with force again.

"Ummmm . . . I like that."

He knew she would, but then he decided to take it down a notch and slide in and out a little at a time, driving her crazy.

"Didn't I tell you to fuck me?" She wanted it fast and furious. "Come on, Zyair, do it like you mean it."

Zyair gave her just what she wanted. A hard, intense fuck. He grabbed onto her waist and pulled her hips toward him, forcing himself deeper and deeper inside her with each thrust.

Either it was Champagne's imagination, or his dick was thicker, longer, and stronger. Her moans were growing louder and louder.

Zyair was covered in sweat, some of it dripping off his body. Normally this would have irritated the hell out of her, but not today.

"I want to come with you inside me," she told him.

He knew she would start playing with her clitoris, and it would be a matter of minutes before she exploded.

Later that night after showering, they went out one last time for drinks and a burger at the midnight grill. They came back to their room and lay in bed discussing all they'd seen so far.

Champagne wondered if this experience would change them as individuals, if it would change their relationship and their sex life would become more exciting and fulfilling as a result.

Not getting that deep with it, Zyair was wondering how he could get Champagne to make love to a woman while they were there. He wanted to bring it up but was apprehensive about how she would react.

Then, suddenly unable to help himself, he blurted out, "Have you ever thought about sleeping with another woman?"

"What?"

"Have you ever thought about—"

"I heard you."

After a couple seconds of silence, Zyair said, "Well?"

"I'm thinking."

"Either you have, or you haven't."

It wasn't that simple because in all actually it really wasn't something she'd given any thought to, aside from her experimenting when she was younger, and that was her secret.

"No, not really."

Disappointed, yet intrigued, he said, "Why not?"

"I don't know. I'm not against it or anything. It's just never been something I was interested in."

"Would you try it?"

Zyair tried to appear blasé with his questioning, but Champagne knew better.

"Why are you asking? Do you want me to? Do you want to have a threesome or something? Is that what this is about? You want to fuck someone else?"

"No, no, I don't want anyone but you, but a brother ain't gonna lie, I'd like to see you with another woman."

Champagne looked over at him. "How long have you been thinking about this?"

"Since we've been together."

"Why bring this up now?"

"Because of where we're at. Because the opportunity may arise. Because we don't know a soul here."

Champagne grew quiet. She was actually considering his words, but fear kept her from voicing it. What came out instead was, "If I agreed to something like that, which I probably wouldn't, who would we get? I can't just be with anyone and I'm not trying to lick any girl's pussy. Plus, I don't even know what kind of woman I would be interested in. Then what if you're attracted to her? What if she wants to have sex with you? I wouldn't be able to handle that. And what if I get turned out."

"What do you mean, what if you get turned out?"

"You know, we both saw *Trois*."

"That's a movie."

"Nah, that shit happens in real life."

"It wouldn't happen to us." Zyair was secure in his spot, at least to the point where he didn't believe a woman could take *his* away.

Champagne looked at him and quoted Cassandra, "Never say never."

CHAPTER EIGHT
"MAN SIZE LOVE"
KLYMAXX

Champagne and Zyair were having the time of their lives. Even when surrounded by others they still enjoyed the comfort of one another. So far the Hedonism experience had been euphoric. It was like one big party, all day and night. They ran across a few other Black couples, although not too many. They were definitely outnumbered by white people.

But here it didn't make much of a difference, because when naked and all walls are down, people tended not to see color. Champagne and Zyair found this fascinating and discussed it amongst themselves several times, wondering why this was the case. Were Blacks more conservative sexually? Were they ashamed of their bodies? Whatever it was, Champagne and Zyair considered themselves the exception to the rule.

Their final night came around leaving them feeling gloomy and sulky. They didn't want to leave but knew they had to. Having been gone for a week, they needed to get home and handle business.

Out for their last drink and far past tipsy, Zyair asked, "Can you believe this is our last night here?"

"I know. I am not looking forward to going home." Champagne had a lot on her plate. She had to find office space, hire an assistant, and get settled with clients. Shaking the thoughts out of her head, she said to Zyair, "Let's do something different and daring."

His ears perked up. "What?"

"Let's make love outside."

"For real?"

"Yeah."

He didn't need to be convinced. He stood up. "When? Now?"

Champagne stood up and laughed. "No, not now. Let's go dancing first."

As they left the area, they passed a table of women. One of them eyed Champagne down. Zyair had noticed her watching them the whole time they were there. He wanted to bring it to Champagne's attention, but decided not to push the issue.

That night while they were on the dance floor, Champagne was pressing her ass up against Zyair when a few things happened all at once. She turned around to kiss him and suddenly felt hands on her hips and breast, pressing up against her back. Startled, she turned around to find an attractive woman dancing a hair's breadth away from her. She was so close, you could feel her body heat.

"I hope you don't mind," the woman said in a slightly husky voice, her lips full and seductive.

Champagne didn't know how to react, and there was an uneasiness in the pit of her stomach.

The woman placed her hands on Champagne's hips. "It's just a dance."

Tipsy and knowing that Zyair was getting turned on

convinced Champagne to throw all caution to the
wind. "I don't mind," she said.

The whole time Zyair had been holding his breath.
This was the girl from the bar. The one that had been
watching them. She was sexy as hell. It was obvious
she was mixed with something other than Black. Her
skin was bronze, and she had short, straight hair that
was cut close. And though small-busted, she had the
biggest nipples he'd ever seen. You could see right
through her blouse.

While he was checking her out, Champagne was
surprising herself, doing the same thing. She felt the
girl's hands wandering from her waist up to her breasts.
Champagne turned around to read Zyair, looked in his
eyes to see if he was experiencing the same sensual
emotions she was.

He noticed a little fear and leaned forward to kiss
her. "Relax," he whispered in her ear. "You're just
dancing. Think of it as foreplay."

She had to admit, she was turned on and her pussy
was becoming lubricated. Champagne found herself
sandwiched between them. She could feel the girl
grinding on her ass. Looking around to see if anyone
was paying them any attention, she wasn't surprised
to find that no one was. This was something that happened a lot on this little island.

Closing her eyes and getting lost in the music,
Champagne, Zyair, and the mysterious woman must
have danced together for over a half an hour. Champagne was so turned on that her pussy hurt. It was
throbbing uncontrollably.

"I'm ready to go," she told Zyair. Facing the woman,
she told her, "Thanks."

The woman grabbed her hands and told her, "Anytime," and kissed her on the lips sensually.

It was a closed-mouth kiss, but the sensation it caused was on a whole other level. Champagne then took Zyair's hands and led him to their room in silence, where she retrieved a blanket.

Zyair was afraid to say a word, not wanting to break Champagne's spell. He could feel the sexual energy radiating off her body and knew tonight's lovemaking would be intense. Not just because of the dance, but it was their last night in Jamaica.

They returned to the beach fully clothed and spread the blanket out. Zyair sat down first, and Champagne sat on his lap, straddling him.

"I love you, you know that, don't you?" Champagne kissed him on the lips."

"I love you too." Zyair grabbed her hips and pressed her into him.

"That was interesting on the dance floor," Champagne said as she ran her hands down Zyair's rippled back.

"Yes, it was. It was sexy. I was ready to take you on the dance floor."

Champagne pressed up against his hardness and smiled. "Yes, I could tell."

Zyair pushed her hips up and pulled up her dress. He linked his fingers underneath her panties. "Let's take these off."

Champagne stood up and let him pull them down.

As she stood close to his face, he took in her scent. Placing his face on her pussy, he pushed her legs open and placed his finger inside her, moving it in a circular motion.

She pressed into his hand. "That feels good."

Zyair removed his finger from inside Champagne. Then he stood up and pulled the dress over Champagne's head. While doing so, he licked her stomach and moved up to her breast. He unsnapped the bra and bit down gently on her nipples.

Once her dress was off, he unzipped his shorts and revealed that he wasn't wearing any underwear. Then he took his shirt off.

Champagne reached out and massaged his dick, which was standing at attention. She got on her knees and started licking the head of his penis, covering the whole length of it with her mouth, running her tongue around it in circular motions.

He loved when she did that. He placed his hands on the back of her head and started moving in her mouth, and Champagne was taking it all in, trying not to let a inch of it out of her mouth. He knew she was trying to make him come, but he wasn't ready for that yet. He pulled away.

"What are you doing? I'm not done yet."

"Let's lay down. I want to taste you."

Not one to turn that down, Champagne stretched out on the blanket.

Zyair pressed her legs open and sat between them. He looked down at her beautiful body. "How did it feel to have your breast caressed by a woman?" He ran his hands down the length of her body, resting between her legs.

With fervor, Champagne took his hand and placed it on her pussy. "It felt soft. I was turned on."

That's what he wanted to hear. Zyair replaced his hand with his mouth and started licking her walls.

Champagne closed her eyes and concentrated on the pleasure that was seeping through her pores. When Zyair placed his tongue on her clitoris, she knew it would be a matter of minutes before she exploded.

Pushing her hips into his mouth and grabbing his

head, she was startled to hear the voice from the disco say, "Can I join in?"

Zyair stopped what he was doing and looked up. Champagne did also. They both saw her standing before them naked.

She looked at Champagne. "My name is Whisper, and I've watched you all day. I want you, not your husband."

Champagne sat up. "I'm not gay."

Whisper laughed and sat down next to them.

By now, Zyair was sitting up, praying silently in his mind that Champagne would say yes. He watched in silence as Champagne's eyes became consumed with desire.

"You don't have to be gay to let me make love to you. I want to taste what your man was tasting. You'll never see me again, I'll never see you again."

Champagne knew this was true. She also knew that Zyair wanted this. This Whisper person did say she wanted her and not him.

Champagne looked over at Zyair, whose eagerness was written all over his face. She decided to throw all caution to the wind. "Yes."

Before Whisper could change her mind, Champagne reached out to her and grazed her lips with her tongue.

Zyair moved over to the side. "I'll watch."

Whisper took Zyair's spot and placed her fingers inside Champagne and licked the juice off. "You taste as good as you look."

Champagne couldn't speak. Her body tingling from head to toe, she was almost shaking.

Whisper told her, "Relax. I'm not here to hurt you, only to please you." Whisper covered Champagne's whole pussy with her mouth and flicked her tongue back and forth, tapping her clitoris.

Please her, she did.

Champagne experienced an orgasm that shook her to the core. It came from every cell in her body. She called out to Zyair, who leaned over and started kissing her in a fit of lust.

Placing her hand on Zyair, Whisper said, "Let me kiss her, let her see what she taste like."

Zyair moved and watched as Champagne devoured Whisper's mouth.

Caught up in the moment, Champagne found herself wanting to taste Whisper, wanting to see what a woman's pussy would feel like on her mouth. She opened her mouth to voice this curiosity, but the words wouldn't come out. What did come out was, "Zyair, I want you inside me *now*."

Whisper nibbled on Champagne's ear and murmured, "Remember me always." She moved over to the side and looked at Zyair. "Can I watch?"

Zyair looked at Champagne, who nodded.

Climbing on top, he entered her with such heat and such passion that Whisper placed her hands on her own pussy and played with her clitoris, bringing herself to orgasm right along with him.

CHAPTER NINE
"MEETING IN THE LADIES ROOM"
KLYMAXX

Champagne lay in the bed and replayed the experience of the night before. She felt like she wanted to do it again, but told herself it was a one-time thing never to happen again. She was even nervous about facing Zyair the next morning.

Fatigued from the lovemaking, Champagne tried to climb out of bed without making a sound. She didn't want to wake Zyair. She headed to the bathroom to masturbate.

Little did she know, he was awake and had been for quite some time. He was replaying the scene over and over in his mind. It was like a movie to him, the way Champagne's body responded to Whisper's touch.

As Zyair watched, his dick got so hard, he thought it was going to explode. Realizing that she was trying to sneak out the bed, he spoke up. "Good morning."

Startled, Champagne walked over to the bed and kissed him on the cheek. "Good morning, sweetie."

Zyair reached for her hand and pulled her back on the bed.

Relunctantly, she sat next to him. "We don't have time to make love again. You know we have to get up and pack."

Zyair sighed. "I know."

"It's back to the real world and away from fantasy island."

Zyair sat up. "Do you want to talk about last night?"

"No. At least not right now."

She needed time to process it, analyze it, replay it over in her mind. She wondered if she was secretly gay, or if she was bisexual. She questioned her actions. Why didn't she push Whisper away? Why was she so turned on? Did she do it for Zyair? Was it the liquor, or was it something she wanted? Had she been in denial all her life? Was she gay as a youngster?

Champagne stood up. "Look, I'm going to take a shower and start packing. While I'm packing, you need to shower. That way we can save time and grab breakfast before we catch the shuttle to the airport."

"We can save more time by showering together," Zyair said, feeling a need to be close to Champagne.

"That's fine."

An hour later they were dressed, packed, and headed to the lounge area for breakfast when, out of the corner of her eye, Champagne caught sight of Whisper talking to one of the workers. Quickly, she averted her attention, but not before glancing her way again.

This time she was busted. Whisper looked at her, winked, and licked her lips.

Either she was crazy, or Champagne got moist.

She grabbed Zyair's hand and started pulling him along.

"Whoa! Whoa! Why are you pulling me? What's the hurry?"

"No hurry. I'm just starving."

The light was streaming through the window when they arrived at Newark Airport. Car service was waiting to take them home. Travel weary, they both slept on the way.

Back at home, they felt lost, displaced, and just plain old out of it. Filled with fever-pitch excitement and exhilaration, the Hedonism vacation was unlike any other they'd taken. Nothing could compare.

To return home to the restaurant and numerous messages on the answering machine from Jackson was anticlimactic and dissatisfying and, in an odd way, made the vacation seem surreal.

The first couple of days, they didn't return any phone calls, but just sat around the house looking at one another. Then that got old and they started to get on with their daily routine.

It'd been a week since their return when Champagne decided to make an appearance at her old job. Damn, she couldn't believe that's what it was now, her old job. Even though she was going on to bigger and better things, change was hard and there was a somberness about the whole thing. After all, she was leaving seven years of her life behind, but she knew in her heart of hearts that she was doing the right thing by making a commitment to herself and her future.

She woke up rejuvenated, focused, and ready to conquer the world. She pulled back the blankets, climbed out the bed, and stretched. Then she went to brush her teeth.

She glanced at the card taped to the mirror and read it out loud: "You can say Good morning, God, or Good God, it's morning." She chose to say, "Good morning, God," and put her focus on making this a productive day. She was going to be the strong one, the one to bite the bullet, the bigger person, and try to draw some kind of truce with Jackson. She didn't want to leave with hatred and dislike on her heart. Life was too short for such bullshit. Plus, Jackson, asshole that he was, had still taught her a lot.

Before leaving the house, Champagne called Zyair for support at the restaurant, only to find he was in a meeting. She then called Alexis.

"Girl, I haven't seen you since you've been back," Alexis told her. "I miss you."

"I was only gone a week."

"Yeah, but a lot can happen in a week."

"Don't I know it."

Champagne thought of Whisper. She wondered whether she should tell Alexis about the escapade. Lord knows, she wanted to, but she didn't feel like being judged. She didn't want to be found out, or be told she was perverted, bisexual, or gay. She didn't want to be labeled or to hear something that would cause her to question herself or her sexuality. Shit! She was doing it enough to herself, and having someone else do it would've been a bit too much.

Sometimes she thought she was going overboard with the constant mind games she played with herself. She tried to just think of it as something that happened. She wanted to just let it be, let it go. Why was she making so much out of it? Why was she blowing it up? She tried convincing herself, "It's something that happened in the heat of the moment, that's all, nothing more, nothing less."

"Want to meet for lunch?" Champagne asked Alexis.

She and Alexis agreed to meet at The Cheesecake Factory, one of their favorite places. Not only for the dessert, which in itself was delectable, but the food was just as delicious. Just thinking about it made her want to hurry up and get going with her day.

When Champagne walked into her former place of employment, all heads turned. She knew they'd heard she was leaving and wanted to jump up and ask her all kinds of questions, but the fear of Jackson and his wrath kept them seated.

"Hi, Champagne," Takia said. "He's in his office. Are you here to ask for your job back?"

Champagne looked at her like she'd lost her mind. "Now you know better than that."

"He's been lost without you, girl," she whispered. "I'm telling you, if you did, you could get whatever you wanted out of him."

"All I really wanted out of him is some respect, and I couldn't even get that."

"We all want that. You know how he—"

Before she could finish, Jackson's office door opened and he looked at Champagne, first with surprise then with contempt. "What are you doing here?"

"Can we step into your office?" Champagne asked, thinking now that this wasn't such a good idea.

Jackson walked into his office, and she followed, closing the door behind her. She waited for him to sit down, he didn't.

"Are you here for your job back?" He hoped so, but of course, he didn't want to tell her that.

"No, I'm here for closure. I'm here to thank you. I'm here because I feel bad about walking out on you the way I did."

"You feel bad? You feel bad?" he asked, his voice getting louder and louder.

Champagne threw her hands up. "Listen, Jackson, I didn't come here for a confrontation. I'm here because I know that you've helped me in my career, because I learned a lot from you, and I thought maybe we could discuss where it—where we went wrong."

"Why do we have to discuss anything? You got too high and mighty. You started thinking you too good for this place."

"That's a lie, and you know it. I got tired of you coming on to me. I got tired of you disrespecting me as a woman. I got tired of you walking around here like king ding-a-ling." Champagne felt like she had nerves of steel, saying what had been in heart for quite some time.

"You never said, 'Hey, Champagne, nice job. Hey, Champagne, I appreciate all you do. No, you just took me for granted."

"You're not a damn child. Why do you want to be praised? This is a job. I'm not raising you or anyone that's up in this joint, and I *am* king ding-a-ling, as you say. This is my ship, and I run it the way I see fit."

"Running it the way you ran it made you lose your best employee, and believe me, I know that's what I was."

Jackson didn't say a word. He knew he was arrogant, and he knew he took advantage of his employees. He also knew what she said was true, but he is who he is.

When he opened his office door and saw Champagne standing there, he seriously hoped she was there for her job back and was ready to offer it to her. Clients had been calling all week, telling him they weren't going to renew their contracts since they'd heard Champagne wasn't there anymore.

"Let me ask you this—How do some of the clients know you quit? Were you planning this all along, a takeover?"

"No, I wasn't planning, and am not planning a takeover. Look around. This is a small office, word gets around. You were yelling and screaming at me my last day here."

Feeling defeated, Jackson sat down. "If I offered you your job back, a partnership, and more money, would you consider it?"

Champagne knew the answer was, "No way in hell," but she told him instead, "I'd think about it. Give me at least a week and I'd get back to you."

"A week is too long."

"Well then, if I have to give you an answer right now, it's no."

Jackson waved her away. "Take a week then."

Champagne turned to leave the office, but she knew she couldn't go out like that, that she shouldn't lead him on. "Jackson, I have to apologize again. I know I'm not coming back here. I'm ready to explore other possibilities, so there's no need to wait on my response."

Before he could say one word, she rushed out of the office and out of the building, with a smile on her face. Champagne felt like a load had been lifted.

Now she was on her way to her favorite place to see her best friend. It couldn't get any better.

When Champagne walked into The Cheesecake Factory, she was disappointed not to see Alexis waiting in front. She glanced around and spotted her. She wasn't sitting by herself, but with a man, dressed in jeans and a T-shirt, muscles bulging in every direction. His arm was resting against the back of Alexis's chair. If she sat any closer to him, she would have been nestled in his arms.

That must be Khalil. Champagne was surprised to feel a pang of jealousy. She thought they were going to have lunch together, just the two of them, and didn't feel like sharing her friend with anyone.

Alexis was so engrossed into whatever this man was telling her that she didn't notice Champagne as she approached. Champagne stood behind her and cleared her throat. "Hello."

Alexis, recognizing the voice, jumped up out of her seat and hugged her. "Hey, girl." Pulling back, she checked her up and down. "You look good. You got a tan and everything. I missed you."

Champagne felt a little better and told her, "I missed you too." She then looked over at the uninvited guest. "Are you going to introduce us?"

Alexis giggled. "This is Khalil, my new man, and this is Champagne, my best friend."

Champagne was surprised to hear her say "my new man." Where did that come from? They'd just met, and she was talking relationship? Weren't things moving a bit fast? She couldn't wait to get Alexis alone. They had some serious talking to do.

Khalil stood up and pulled the chair out for Champagne, who did take note that, at least, he was a gentleman.

"It's nice meeting you," he said. "I've heard so much about you."

"In a week's time? Wow! I wish I knew more about you." Champagne didn't know what was wrong with her, but she just had to be bitchy.

Alexis noticed it right away and stood up. "I'm going to the ladies' room. Champagne, you care to join me?"

The way Alexis looked at her, Champagne knew she'd better join her.

When they walked inside, there were a couple of women washing their hands. Alexis waited until they walked out and tore into Champagne. "What the hell is that all about?"

Her tone threw Champagne off balance. "What are you talking about?"

"You know what I'm about. I'm talking about your rudeness and your scrutiny. I'm talking about you acting like you don't like Khalil and you don't even know him."

Champagne knew she was right. All she could do was apologize and be honest. "I'm sorry. I thought it would just be you and I meeting. I thought I'd have you all to myself."

Alexis pulled Champagne into her arms. "That's so sweet, and I know you mean well. But, baby, I'm into this man, and I just wanted y'all to meet."

Champagne pulled away. "You really into him?"

"Yeah."

"You don't think this is moving a bit fast?"

"Maybe. But I'm tired of being by myself, of not having any companionship."

"Well, do you think it's wise to jump into a relationship just because you're tired of being lonely?"

Alexis rolled her eyes. "Why are you hating on a sister?"

"I'm not hating. I'm just saying, you don't want to hop into a relationship just because . . ."

"It's not just because. Listen, I appreciate your concern, but you have a man. I've finally got one too. I enjoy his company, and he enjoys mine. You should be happy for me."

There was really nothing left for Champagne to say. Alexis was going to do what she wanted to do anyway.

"Okay, let's do this," Champagne suggested. "Let's go back to the table and start all over. I promise, I won't be an asshole."

"You promise?"

Champagne took her hand, and together they walked out the bathroom.

CHAPTER TEN
"GIVE IT TO ME BABY"
RICK JAMES

Later that night Champagne waited for Zyair to come home. She couldn't wait to tell him about Khalil. She was hoping to convince Zyair to investigate him. She knew he did it with his employees, so why wouldn't he do it for her friend?

"Are you crazy?" he asked her. "What are you thinking of, invading someone's privacy like that?"

"Well, you do it for your employees."

"That's different. That's because they'll be working for me, handling my money."

"But she's my best friend. I'm worried about her."

"She's a grown-ass woman, Champagne."

Champagne felt like he wasn't even trying to understand. She wanted him to get that the reason she was concerned is because Alexis just met this guy and for her to be calling him her man so soon just didn't sit right with Champagne. As a matter of fact, he didn't fit right to her either. There was something about him that just really bothered her. She didn't know what it was, but whatever it was, she was going to find out one way or another, with or without Zyair's help.

"You don't think you're just jealous?" Zyair asked.

"Why the heck would I be jealous?"

"Because you think you're going to lose your best friend."

Champagne rolled her eyes.

"It was just a thought."

Champagne knew there was some truth to it, that there was more than a slight chance that he was right. After all, Alexis was her best friend and had always been available to her. Whenever she wanted to do something, or needed someone to talk to, all she had to do was pick up the phone and Alexis was there.

The more Champagne thought about it, the more messed up she felt. She now saw how much she bene-fited from her friend being single. How messed up was that? Champagne also recalled the many occasions Alexis wanted to spend time with her and she was un-able to, because Zyair had made plans.

She recalled the saying that some people take com-fort in another's misery. She hoped she wasn't that type of person. Champagne knew she should be happy for Alexis. It was about time she got involved with someone. She just didn't want things to change, and she knew they would. So before Khalil took Alexis away, Champagne was going to look into his back-ground and make sure he was worthy of her.

She knew she was wrong, but she convinced herself that it would be worth it, should something pop up. If it didn't, that would be even better, because then they could do things together as couples.

Champagne told Zyair, "You know what, sweetie, it's not my business. I'm reading way more into this than I should. And not only that, who's to say that's it going to last?"

"Good. What you need to be doing, instead of thinking about Alexis and her new man, is focusing on your new business. You know you're about to start your interviewing process. Why don't you get together your list of questions?"

Champagne knew Zyair was right once again, and she planned on doing just that in the morning, after she was well rested and she could concentrate on what she was doing.

Later that night Champagne was awakened by Zyair's touch as he pressed up against her ass. She turned over and touched his face.

"What were you dreaming about?" he asked. "You were moaning and playing with yourself."

"Get out of here." Champagne recalled that she was having a sexy-ass dream, but there was no way in hell she was playing with herself.

"No, for real, you were."

Damn, she was busted. She was dreaming that she was making love to a woman. Was she that turned-on that it was affecting her sleep? Reality had set in. She realized that it wasn't only in her waking hours that she thought about her sexual escapade in Hedonism. She was consumed with it day and night. She tried to tell herself that what happened was a one-time thing, but she was slowly starting to think it went far deeper than that.

That night in Hedonism stirred something up in her. Another person might say it brought out the freak in her. She didn't know what it meant. All she knew for certain was that she wanted to try it again.

Why? Why her? Other than the fact that the way Whisper caressed her, kissed her, and put her lips on her pussy made her feel good. Or was it the way Whisper was certain of herself and her skills? There was a tenderness about it, something she'd never experienced before.

Now, don't get her wrong, Champagne felt these things from Zyair, but this was on another level. They say, women know what women want, when they want it, and how they want it. Well, it sure seemed like it, because the way Whisper made love to her pussy, devouring it like it was the best dessert she ever had, still had her thinking, wishing, and wanting.

They, whoever they are, also say that women have a deeper understanding of each other in and out of bed. Champagne couldn't verify any of that on a relationship level, but she could on a friendship level because sometimes when she was going through it or having a moment and Zyair couldn't relate, she would call Alexis, who would know instantly what to say or what to do about it.

Damn, why was this consuming her? She wished she had someone she could talk to about it, spill her desires out to without being judged, but there was no one. She definitely wasn't going to tell Alexis.

"So," Zyair said, interrupting her thoughts, "what were you dreaming about?"

Champagne decided to be honest. What the heck! What is he going to do or say, other than have more questions or want details? "I was dreaming about sex . . . sex with a woman."

Champagne could read the interest on Zyair's face as he moved closer to her. If he got any closer, he would have been inside her.

"Want to tell me about it?"

Champagne recalled the details, but she just didn't want to give them up. What she was willing to give up, though, was the fact that she'd been having these thoughts a lot lately. "I don't really remember the details." Champagne saw the look of disappointment on Zyair's face. "Zyair?"

"Yes?" There was hope in his voice.

"I know that we're trying to better our relationship, and I also know that the only way to do that is with honesty."

On the honesty note, Zyair sat up again and braced himself. He was starting to get nervous. When someone started talking about honesty in a relationship, you couldn't help but wonder where they were going with this. He wanted to rush her along and make her get to whatever point she was trying to make, to say whatever she had to say, so he could deal with it.

"Go on."

Laying on her back, looking up at the ceiling, Champagne said, "I think I might want to try, I might want to, um . . ." Damn, how come she couldn't just say it? Why couldn't she just say she wanted to be with a woman again, and not while intoxicated? She wanted to be sure that she enjoyed it as much as she remembered.

Zyair seemed so interested in her dream that she hoped he'd be like, "Good. Let's do this," or maybe it was just something he wanted to see once more. Maybe this time around he would want to take part in it, and that wasn't something she felt she could handle. If he said yes, would theirs now be an open relationship? Was an open relationship something she wanted? What would it consist of? Would he be sleeping with other women? Would he go down on them?

After thinking it over, Champagne was pissed she even opened her mouth.

Growing more anxious by the moment, Zyair told

her, "Go on and say it. Say what's on your mind. I love you no matter—"

Before he could finish, Champagne said, "I want to sleep with another woman." There she'd said it and couldn't take it back. Would she regret it? She didn't know why she even felt the need to tell him? Maybe she should have kept it to herself and did this on her own, but she didn't want to sneak though.

"You want to what?" This is definitely not what he was expecting her to say.

Champagne covered her face. "You know what? Never mind. Forget I said anything."

The last thing Zyair wanted Champagne to do was close down. He removed her hands. "There's no need to take it back. I want whatever you want. I want for us to try new things. I want for us to be able to tell each other our fantasies. I don't want to have any secrets."

Champagne started to interrupt, but Zyair was on a roll.

"I want for us to be best friends again. Somehow we've lost that. How are we going to do that if we can't say what's on our mind? I want us to be able to say anything and everything to one another without the judgment. Like I said, I want what you want, even if that's to bring another woman in our bed for us."

Okay, okay, he was getting the wrong impression. She wasn't talking about bringing another woman into the relationship or into their bed for them, but for herself. It sounded like that's what he thought she meant, so Champagne knew she had to clarify that right away.

She sat up. "Hold up, hold up, hold up. I didn't say anything about bring another female in our bed for us."

Confused and disappointed, Zyair thought he was going to have is cake and eat it too. He asked her, "Well, what did you mean?"

"I guess what I'm asking you is to do what we did in Jamaica, but not under those conditions, not under the influence. I want to see if I enjoyed it as much as I did for myself, and not because of you."

"Would that be so bad, enjoying it because you were under the influence?" Zyair asked.

For a brief second a shot of insecurity swept through him. What the hell did that girl do to his woman? Did that Whisper put it down like that? Was she that good that Champagne was thinking about it a week later? Zyair knew his pussy-eating skills were up to par, but was he building himself up? Nah, there was no ways he was as good as he was only in his mind. No way in hell. After all these years, he knew that Champagne couldn't be faking her pleasure.

He couldn't help it. He just had to know. "What about it did you enjoy? Was she better than me? Did she make you come harder?"

Champagne could tell immediately where these questions were coming from—his insecurity—and didn't want to take it there. She touched his arm. "Sweetie, it's not that serious. And if you're going to start doubting us and how you make love to me, then let's just forget I said anything."

Okay, he messed up and he knew it. He didn't want her to change her mind, because although he may have jumped to conclusions thinking she'd let him be a part of the next escapade, he was more than willing to watch once again.

"No, no, I don't doubt us. That's not it at all. It's just that we never talked about what happened. Whenever

I brought it up, you nixed it off or changed the subject."

His statement was correct. She did want to pretend that none of it happened. That obviously didn't work because it was still on her mind. She now wanted to close the subject, and turn over and go back to sleep, but she knew that wouldn't happen now.

"Okay, well let's talk about it now. What do you want to know?"

Zyair looked her in the eyes. "Did it feel good?"

"Yes."

"Did it feel different from when I make love to you?"

"Different yes, better no. And if you recall, we made love immediately after, and it intensified our lovemaking."

"What was different about it?"

"About what? Us?"

"No. You and her."

"You know how they say a woman's touch is softer, gentler?"

"Yes."

"Well, it's sort of true. There was sensuality there that I hadn't experienced before, a sort of sexiness that only women have." Seeing the confused look on his face, she knew she had to stroke his ego. "It doesn't take away from what you and I have, though."

"What turned you on most about her?

To this question Champagne smiled and answered, "Her breast." She touched her own as she said this, and Zyair took notice.

Champagne had discovered she was a breast girl. She found herself looking at women when she shouldn't be, her eyes almost always wandering to breast level. One thing she was certain of, the next time the occasion rose she was going to be a bit more aggressive. She was going to reach out and touch. Was she going to go down on a woman? That she couldn't attest to, but one never knows.

"How did she eat your pussy?"

Champagne looked at him and wondered if she wanted to go there. *What the heck! I might as well. After all, I might get a treat afterwards.*

"How did she eat my pussy? You want me to tell you or show you?"

Zyair immediately got hard. "How are you going to show me?"

"I'll instruct."

Zyair climbed out the bed and pulled off his briefs, and Champagne slid out of her gown, which was all she was wearing.

Champagne was wet and ready. "Kiss me," she told him as she straddled him, his dick sliding in her. She wanted to be on top, so she could be in control. She also wanted to sit on his face. Yes, that's how she wanted him to eat her out.

Zyair placed his lips on hers and started to tease her with his tongue.

She pulled her mouth away from his and sat up straighter. She placed her hands on his chest, bent over slightly, raising her pussy up slowly to the tip of his dick, and slammed down. Champagne, feeling aggressive, did this a few more times. "You like it?" she asked.

All Zyair could do is moan. He tried to reach out and grab her hips, but she pushed his hands back down and continued to ride him at a slow pace, torturing him.

"Go faster," he told her.

"No, let me do this my way." Champagne then pressed down as hard as she could and started rocking back and forth. "Damn, this feels good," she said, getting lost in her own world.

Zyair could feel his orgasm building up, but it was too soon for him. He wasn't ready to come just yet. "Come on," he said, "let me eat that pussy."

Champagne slid off him and straddled his face.

"Tell me how you want it," he told her.

On her knees over his face, Champagne spread her pussy lips open and told him, "Lick the walls. I want you to taste every inch."

Zyair grabbed her buttocks and pulled her to his mouth. Then he put his tongue in as far as it would go.

Champagne started pressing into his mouth, trying to feel every movement, every inch of his tongue. Eventually she had to bend over and balance herself on her hands, while he devoured her.

Zyair then placed his entire mouth over her pussy, and started moving his tongue back and forth against her clitoris.

"Yes, yes, that's it," Champagne said, feeling so close to coming. "Put your finger inside me."

Zyair did as she requested and started moving his finger in and out real slow.

Champagne, lost in the pleasure, started to grind and grind. "Shit, you're going to make me come too fast." She sat up straight, grabbed her titties, and started squeezing her nipples.

All the while, Zyair was watching her. It'd been a long time since he'd seen her so animated.

Right at this moment, Zyair felt like the muthafuckin' man, and when she screamed out and told him to taste her and he placed his tongue deep inside her walls, he knew that he was.

After she was done coming, Champagne immediately

wanted him inside her. She climbed on him again, this time her back facing him, and rode him at a fast pace while touching her clitoris. She wanted another orgasm and wanted Zyair to get his as well.

It didn't take long for Zyair to grab her hips and press up inside her. "Ahhhh," was all he could manage to say as he exploded inside her.

When he was at the end of his orgasm, Champagne had hers. She threw her head back and yelled out, "Shit!" She climbed off him and collapsed in his arms.

"I love you," he told her.

Kissing him, she told him she loved him as well and they both fell asleep.

The next morning, Zyair ruined the whole aftersex mood, asking her, "If I agree to do this again, what will I get out of it?"

Champagne just looked at him like he was crazy and started to get out of the bed. After all, he was the one that started all this shit. "You know what, Zyair . . . let's just forget the whole thing."

Not understanding what he did wrong, he grabbed her arm and said, "Wait, wait. What's wrong?"

Champagne looked at him in disbelief. She just shook her head. *How could he not know what's wrong?*

"Champagne, talk to me," Zyair begged.

"You want to know what's wrong? I'll tell you what's wrong. What's wrong is the fact that this was your idea in the first place, the whole 'let me see you make love with a woman.' I did that shit for you and now, because I enjoyed it and want to try it again, you're tripping. You're trying to change shit all up."

What could he say? She was right. It was his idea. They'd never said it would be a one-time thing, but they'd never said they'd have a repeat session either.

They'd just jumped into it headfirst. "I apologize," he told her. "I didn't mean that the way it came out."

Champagne didn't want to hear any apologies. She put her hands on her hips. "And what do you mean, what do you get out to the deal? What do you want to get out the deal? More pussy? A new pussy? Is that it? Is that what you want?"

That's what you wanted, he thought to himself, but didn't dare say it out loud. Zyair glanced at the clock. He realized he needed to get up and get dressed. Plus, he didn't feel like having this conversation. "Champagne, the only pussy I want is yours."

Champagne didn't know whether to believe him or not, knowing she wouldn't get a straight answer and not wanting to hear him say, "Yeah, I want some new pussy," she decided to end this conversation. "You know what, let's just forget the whole thing. You have to work, and I have things to do today. Let's just get dressed and get on with our day."

Zyair didn't want to start his day on a negative note. He didn't want to forget the whole thing, but he knew not to press the subject just yet. "Okay, how about we try this? Let's take a day and think about everything we've talked about and put together a list of rules. The rules will consist of things that are acceptable and things that aren't. That's the only way we're going to go through with this."

Champagne really didn't want to agree because she was afraid of what might be on his list. She wasn't sure if she could handle it, but she agreed to it anyway. At least this way, she'd know where his head was.

CHAPTER ELEVEN
"WHAT'S GOING ON"
MARVIN GAYE

Zyair shot the ball through the hoops. He was out with his boys, and they were wrapping up a game of two on two.

"So, what's up?" Thomas asked him as they settled on the bench. "Are we going to catch a bite to eat or what?"

"Let me call Champagne and see if she's cooking today."

"See, man, you're lucky as hell. A home-cooked meal. Maybe I could come over for dinner."

Zyair didn't want to tell Thomas that there was no way Champagne was letting him come and eat her precious food, at least not today. She was still pissed off at him, and from experience, he knew she could hold a grudge.

Since the incident that put her in that space with Thomas had just happened a week ago, it would be at least another two weeks before she even allowed him to eat her food.

Zyair, Thomas, Harrison, and Judge went out to a

strip club the week before, and Zyair had to admit, a good time was had by all. Champagne never asked where they were going or what they did. There seemed to be little concern on her part. Zyair felt like a lucky man. He'd re-earned her trust, or so he thought.

To Champagne, it just took up too much energy to wonder what he was doing when he was out with his boys. If she did that, it could and would drive her crazy. It did once before, and she didn't want to go that route again. She decided to let his past infidelity be just that, a thing of the past. After all it was years ago, and it had taken her quite some time to get to this point.

Shit, from experience she'd learned that if you search you will find, and that when you go looking, you had to be prepared for any and everything. That's how she'd found out he was cheating before, by snooping. What made it so bad was that this was the only time she'd followed him around.

She felt at the time that she had the right. Zyair wasn't being as attentive as he normally was. They were into year two of their relationship and had settled into a routine, sort of like their current circumstance. The phone calls every few hours had stopped. The "I'm just checking on you to see if you need anything" had stopped. The "I just want to spend time with you, and let's have lunch together" had stopped. Even the good-night phone calls.

On top of all that, the sex was almost non-existent, and the oral had dwindled. He no longer took the time to feel her, to smell her, lick her and be one with the pussy. Instead he would go straight for the clit, plucking it like it was a chord, like he was thinking, *Okay, let me hurry up and make her come so I can get mine.*

Now this stuff, she could have let slipped by a little,

because she knew and understood that relationships often went through its peaks and valleys, its highs and lows. She'd decided that's what was happening, and a little more work and a lot more conversation could turn it around.

What made Champagne doubt this concept and think a little more was going on than she wanted to admit was the constant phone calls from his friend Divine.

Zyair was hosting an event for her company, which was just starting up. She was calling him an awful lot, more so than any of his other clients. It seemed like seventy-five percent of the time when the phone rang it was her. Champagne was a little bothered by it, and she let him know. Of course, he told her she was imagining things.

But being a woman, Champagne knew she wasn't crazy. She felt it in her gut that this chick wanted her man, and once again when she brought it to Zyair's attention, he dismissed it.

Well, late one night Divine called. Champagne listened while Zyair talked to her. The conversation sounded more personal than business.

The second they got off the phone, Champagne asked, "What the hell was that about?"

"Oh, she's just going through some things right now and needed to discuss them with someone," he told her.

"Well, she need to discuss the shit with someone other than you. You're doing business with her, you're not her damn friend."

What Champagne didn't know was that Zyair and this Divine chick grew up together. For some reason he'd withheld this information from her, and you know when information is withheld there's always more to the story.

Champagne ended up finding out from Thomas. Yep, he was always involved in some shit. She'd overheard him and Zyair talking. They were sitting in the kitchen and Champagne had just walked in the room.

"Man, I saw Divine the other day. She's come a long way since college. She's looking good, man."

Champagne turned around in time to see Zyair giving Thomas a look. Of course, she couldn't let that go. "What's going on?"

Zyair had this real dumb look on his face. "What are you talking about?"

Champagne put her hands on her hips. "Thomas is talking like you both knew her in your past."

Zyair knew he was busted. He didn't know why he just didn't tell her from gate that Divine was an old friend. He tried to play it off by sounding nonchalant. "Oh, I thought I told you we went to school together."

Champagne politely asked Thomas to leave, before ripping Zyair a new asshole. That night he slept in the spare bedroom.

Over the next few weeks, Champagne found herself going through his pockets, looking at his calendar, doing things that were so out of character for her. But she couldn't help herself, she was out of control. She had to know if her gut instinct was right.

One night while Zyair was asleep, she got hold of his cell phone and figured out his pass code, which wasn't too hard, seeing most men used either their birth date or numbers from their social security number for their code. Well, she found the evidence she was looking for.

On his voicemail was a message from Divine expressing how wonderful last night had been, even if it was a mistake. She expressed her feelings for him and asked him, didn't he know how good they could be together, in and out of bed, and to please give her a chance.

Unable to take anymore, Champagne went into the bedroom and woke Zyair up by pushing him off the bed.

"What the—?"

"I knew it, I knew it," Champagne ranted and raved. She shoved the phone in his face. "You tried to play me. How could you do this to me?"

Of course, he tried to act like he didn't know what she was talking about.

"Please, Zyair, don't play dumb with me. You've played me enough. I heard your little love message."

Zyair took the phone out of her hand and retrieved the message. As he listened, Champagne grabbed her belongings and started to leave.

Jumping up out of the bed, he apologized and apologized. He begged her to stay, saying he could explain, that it only happened one time.

Well, once was enough. She left him.

Zyair did everything in his power to get her back. He begged, sent flowers, kept showing up at her office at her house, discontinued all business with Divine, and lost money because of it.

Eventually Champagne forgave him and returned.

Thomas knew about the affair, and even though his loyalty lay with Zyair, she couldn't help but feel like he should have stopped him. After all, she was the one that helped him get his endorsement deal, she was the one that, when he got into a bad accident, assisted Zyair in taking care of him. She was the one that cooked for him and thought of him like extended family. That had changed over the years, though, because whenever something went down, Thomas either knew about it, was around, or was a part of it.

The night when Zyair got ready to leave she actually asked him where they were going and he told her, "To a strip club."

She wanted to ask if she could go as well, but she knew better. One, he was going with his boys, and two, it would give away the fact that the conversation they had earlier that week, the whole sex-with-a-female thing, was still on her mind.

That night at the strip club, Zyair and his boys were drinking and taking in the scenery when two strippers approached them and asked if anyone wanted a lap dance. Normally this was something Zyair didn't do, but after one too many drinks and seeing that the other fellows were with it, he decided, what the hell. Simply put, Zyair got caught up in the moment.

The next day they were all at his house watching a game. Champagne was with a client at a premiere, so they had the house to themselves. Harrison started joking with Zyair, "Yo, man, you should have seen your face when that girl was all on you."

Thomas laughed. "See, that's just what a man needs, a lap dance at the end of the day."

Once again Champagne walked in when Thomas was opening his mouth. Everyone shut up immediately when she gave them all the evil eye.

"So, you didn't tell me you got a lap dance, Zyair." That's right, Champagne was putting his ass on blast in front of all his boys.

"Um-um, Champagne," Thomas said, trying to break the tension, "it was his first time. We thought it would be a good joke."

Champagne gave him the look and said, "Oh really?"

Two minutes later his boys were all leaving. Champagne went upstairs without saying a word, leaving Zyair sitting on the couch waiting for the damn to burst.

Champagne didn't know if she was angry, aggravated, or what. She took a quick shower and decided to confront him on the lap dance.

Zyair hadn't moved from the spot he was in. He was still watching the game.

"So you got a lap dance, huh? You let some stank-ass ho that's been dancin' all night, niggas been feelin' all up on her, lookin' in her pussy—she was probably all sweaty and shit—and you let her get on you?"

Damn! When she said it that way, Zyair felt disgusted with himself. There was no way he could deny it, because she'd heard what she heard.

He decided to just make her understand that it really wasn't that serious, that all the other fellas were doing it, and that the truth of the matter was that he really didn't derive any pleasure from it.

"You expect me to believe that?" she asked.

He knew she wouldn't, but it was still halfway truthful. The excitement of a honey rubbing up against him was exciting for a second, but then after looking around and seeing that numerous other people were getting the same thing done, and wondering how many people she'd been up on put a damper on the mood for him. It didn't soften his hard-on now, but mentally he wasn't there. So instead of saying another word, he decided to suck it up and take the cursing out. He was wrong and he knew it.

So here Zyair and Thomas sat, Thomas wanting to come over for dinner, that is, if Champagne was cooking, and Zyair knowing damn well that, even if she was, he wouldn't be welcome. As a matter of fact, he wouldn't be welcome for a hot moment.

Deciding to change the subject, Zyair looked around to make sure no one was within listening distance. "So, what do you think of open relationships?"

Thomas raised his eyebrows. "Why are you asking me that? I know you and Champagne ain't thinking about no shit like that." He thought Zyair would be out of his mind to even consider it. There was no way in the world, he would let another man get all up in his. No way in hell.

"Nah, man, I was just asking, trying to get your opinion."

"Why would you want my opinion on something like that?"

"Just trying to make conversation. Damn! I overheard two of my employees talking about it."

Thomas didn't believe a word Zyair was saying. For one, Zyair never talked about his employees. I mean, he didn't really befriend them like that, and Thomas was having a hard time believing Zyair would eavesdrop. He just wasn't that type of man.

Thomas knew something was up, but if Zyair wanted to play the conversation this way, he'd let him. He knew Zyair too well to believe this was some hypothetical.

Damn, Thomas thought, *I never would've thought Champagne had the freak in her like that, but shit, one never knows. Zyair's a lucky man. He's got a lady in the streets and a freak in—*

"Well, what do you think about it?"

"What specifically are you asking me?"

Ready to let it go, Zyair told him, "I'm asking you about open relationships—switching, swinging, threesomes."

Thomas nudged Zyair. "Come on, come clean with me. You and Champagne, y'all into that? Is that what this is about?"

Zyair didn't know how much he wanted to tell Thomas, because Thomas sometimes blurted things out. "I'm just curious."

"What? You ain't satisfied with Champagne?"

"That's not what I'm saying. It's just that after listening to my employees it got me to thinking."

"Boy, don't fuck up what you have. You know you almost lost her once and you damn near went out your mind."

"I ain't gonna mess up. Just humor me. Damn! You're getting all emotional over my issue."

After looking at Zyair for a second or two, Thomas said, "Man, I don't know. Even though you're just saying you're curious, I don't really see Champagne being down with something like that. I'll say this, though—If I had a woman and that was something I might could get away with, I would. I'm only talking about the threesome thing, the having two women—hell yeah. But the whole swinging aspect of it, letting another man get with mine, oh hell no."

Zyair laughed. That's definitely not what he was talking about. After ending the conversation, Zyair called Champagne to see if she was cooking.

She was, and Thomas was not invited.

CHAPTER TWELVE
"I'M EVERY WOMAN"
CHAKA KHAN

Champagne stood at the door of her new office and felt an overwhelming sense of pride, and fear. Pride because she was going out on her own and fulfilling a dream, making an idea a reality, fear because she had no idea how this would turn out. She knew she was more than capable of doing the job, or running her own business. She knew her skills were up to par and she also knew that if she didn't know what to do about something, she could figure it out. She knew she had the goods to deliver. It's not like she was a novice in her field, she was one of the best.

Unlocking the door and taking the first step was an emotional event. Personal Touch, Inc. was her very own place of business, and that's just what she planned on giving each and everyone of her clients. She would treat each and everyone of them like they were her only clients. She knew that's what everyone said, especially when they were starting a service-based business, and it often started that way, only to wear off. But she'd vowed to offer a service with integrity.

Because she had some money saved and Zyair had fronted her what was considered an investment, she would be able to hire a secretary/receptionist and an assistant. The secretary would be there to type letters, brochures, make appointments, things that could be done in-house. The assistant would be someone that could run errands and assist in the handling of clients, someone she could depend on.

Zyair asked her, "Are you looking for somebody with experience, or somebody new to this business?"

"I'm looking for someone new and hungry, someone eager to learn, someone willing to grow with me, not someone who thought they knew more than me."

When Zyair wrote out the check to her, she kept thanking him for the loan. Finally, after going back and forth about the money she decided to listen when he said, "Just take the damn money, girl. It's an investment in our future together."

After listening numerous times to Champagne talking about how she wanted to do this on her own, Alexis told her, "Girl, your man loves you. He worships the ground you walk on, and with him helping financially, you will have a leg up on other businesses just starting out. What you need to do is be thankful for his generosity and that you have a man that has the money to help you fund your dream. Shit, this will allow you to hire people and everything."

When Alexis, the one who never cursed said, "Shit," Champagne almost passed out. This was another sign of Khalil being a bad influence. Alexis had even started to dress sexier. Her clothes were getting a little tighter, and she even showed cleavage a little more now. Champagne knew that these changes had to do with him, but that was neither here nor there. Now was not the time to concentrate and worry about what Alexis was doing. What she needed to do was get prepared for the interviews she had lined up.

There was a coffee shop right down stairs and the plan was to meet the prospective employees at the office and if she liked them, they would go downstairs and continue the interview. If the first impression was one she didn't like, she'd wrap it up and send them on their way.

Glancing at her watch, Champagne noticed she had about thirty minutes before her first interview. There would be four interviews. Zyair told her she was taking on a lot, but she knew that she could handle it. All she had to do was pace herself. Her first interview was scheduled for 10:00 a.m., and she had them scheduled an hour and a half apart, her last interview coming up at 2:30. Okay, maybe she did bite off more than she could chew.

Champagne walked into the office, which had three rooms to it, the reception area, a small office for her assistant, and a much larger office, her space. Her office faced the front of the building and when she looked out the window, she could see the goings-on on the street below.

Champagne couldn't wait to furnish her office. She'd already chosen her colors, different shades of blue. She even had one of her past artist clients coming to paint a mural of a sunset for her. Thankfully her career choice was a creative one, and it allowed her to not be stuffy or have a conservative work space.

Tomorrow she would go out and start looking for furniture. She'd concentrate on her office first because she anticipated it being her home away from home. For the reception and assistant areas she would get the basics. Maybe later down the road, when she was a little more established, she'd go splurge.

Today for the interviews she had two chairs facing one another and a table, where they could fill out a personality questionnaire. She wanted everyone that would be working with and for her to vibe. She wasn't sure if this personality test thing would work, but she was going to find out.

She'd already put the coffee shop on alert that she would be coming and going.

The interviewing in the coffee shop was Zyair's idea. He told her, "When you interview in a more relaxed and casual environment, people tend to let their guard down, and are more themselves."

Not one to doubt a man with a successful business, she decided to take his word and was glad that she did.

Shanese, her first interviewee, although a college graduate, was as hood as they come.

Champagne thought, *You can take the girl out the hood, but you can't take the hood out of the girl*.

Shanese twisted her neck and chewed gum when answering questions.

Not even ten minutes had gone by before Champagne made the decision to end the interview right then and there and educate a sister. She knew she wouldn't be hiring her, but she didn't want her to go out into the world and play herself. Champagne believed that sisters had to support one another, encourage one another, advise one another, and pull each other up if they were in the position to do so.

"Listen," Champagne told her, "I don't want you to get offended by what I'm about to say, but I'm trying to help you." Champagne could see Shanese's guard go up immediately. "I'm not going to hire you, and this is why. From one sister to another, when you go out on interviews, you need to be more professional. You need to step up your presentation. On interviews first impressions are important."

When Shanese didn't say anything, Champagne asked her, "You want me to go on?"

Appreciative, Shanese told her, "Yes."

"Okay, first of all you shouldn't lean back in the chair like you're chillin'."

Shanese sat up.

"The chewing gum, that's a definite no-no. Take the gum out of your mouth before you get to the interview, and no matter what kind of interview you're going on, you should always dress professional."

"What are you saying?" Shanese asked. "Are you saying that I have to wear a suit?"

"A suit would be nice, but if you don't have one, a skirt and blouse with some pumps."

Shanese, although disappointed that she didn't get the job, appreciated what Champagne was telling her. She stood up and put out her hand. "Thanks for caring enough to tell me the truth."

Champagne ignored her hand and pulled out her arms to hug her. "Have faith, and you're welcome. I'm only trying to help you, not hurt you. Shanese, even if you're not real experienced, you want to make the person that's interviewing feel like they wouldn't mind taking the time out to train you. You need to do your best to impress them."

Shanese thanked her again before leaving.

None of the interviewees worked out. Either they didn't have the type of energy she was looking for, or they wanted too much money. After the last interview, Champagne decided she'd stop by Private Affairs and see what Zyair was up to, but not before going to this new furniture spot she'd heard about that was owned by two gay men. She'd overheard two women discussing how they could go broke in there, that the furniture was eclectic, yet natural.

She definitely didn't want to go broke, but she was prepared to spend a little money. Champagne wanted a different feel to her office. She didn't want the typical desk, chair, and loveseat, but was aiming for comfort and relaxation. She wanted her clients to come in and feel at home, not feel like they were being interviewed or put on display. After all, her business dealt with personalities, and she wanted her surroundings to reflect that.

When Champagne pulled into the parking lot, she noticed Thomas standing by a Lexus convertible. He appeared to be in a heated conversation with some guy. She had to look twice because the guy looked very familiar, but she couldn't place him.

Climbing out of her car, she grabbed her purse and locked the door behind her. She wanted to get into the store without Thomas seeing her, but just as she was opening the door, she heard her name being called.

"Champagne, hold up!"

Damn! She turned around and saw Thomas walking her way.

"What are you doing on this side of town?"

"Shopping for my new office."

"Oh, congratulations! Zyair told me all about it. He's so proud of you."

"Thanks."

"So how's your friend, Alexis?"

Champagne tried her best not to roll her eyes.

Thomas was always asking about her. She'd already told him she wasn't hooking them up. Plus, he wasn't Alexis's type anyway. But now, with her dating Khalil, Champagne didn't know what or who she would be attracted to. "Thomas, you need to give that fantasy up. Alexis has a man now, and I think they're serious."

Thomas frowned. "She has a what?" His attraction to Alexis was serious. He wondered how he could convince Champagne that he was ready to let go of his doggish ways to be with Alexis. He wanted her to know that he was aware of the fact that Alexis was a dime and deserved to be treated as such. Now here Champagne stood, crushing his heart with the information that Alexis had a man. Oh hell no, he needed to find out more information.

"A man. I didn't stutter." Champagne was amused by the look on Thomas's face. He looked as though his feelings were hurt for real.

"Who? What's his name?"

"Khalil."

"Who the hell is he? Where's he from?"

"He's new in town." Champagne was ready to wrap up this conversation. She glanced at her watch. "Other than that, I don't know much about him."

"What do you mean, you don't know much about him? That's your girl. You need to find out more information."

When he said that, Champagne knew she'd found the right one to look into Khalil's background, but would he do it without Zyair finding out? She needed to think on that one before saying anything to him.

"That's what I'm trying to do, Thomas." She glanced at her watch once more. "Listen, I've got to go, but we'll talk more later." She just turned and walked away without even waiting for him to say goodbye.

Thomas watched her as she swayed her way into the building. He couldn't help recalling the conversation he and Zyair had. "Uh-huh-huh," he said to himself, you just never know which ones are turned out."

CHAPTER THIRTEEN

"FREAK LIKE ME"

ADINA HOWARD

Champagne sat in Zyair's office as she waited for him to finish talking to his cook. After leaving the furniture store, she'd called him up and told him she felt like doing something, hanging out. He agreed. They hadn't made a decision where they would be going. The only thing they knew was that they would do something out of the ordinary, something different.

Champagne knew that they weren't really into the club scene, but a dance or two might be nice. Shit, it'd been a while since she shook her ass, but then again, after taking into consideration the way women danced now, especially in videos, ass popping, titties shaking, maybe that was a good thing.

"Do you have anything in particular you'd like to do?" she asked Zyair, before he left the office.

"Nothing comes to mind. You decide, and when I come back, let me know."

Well, he'd been gone now for a full fifteen minutes and she was getting anxious. Especially since she'd made the decision where she wanted to go. Boy, would he be surprised. How was she going to tell him that she wanted to go to a strip club to see some naked ass? He'd probably think, *Here we go again.* How was she going to tell him that even though she was pissed at him for getting a lap dance? After thinking about it, not only did it turn her on, but now she found herself wanting one. Champagne knew that sounded hypo-critical, but it was what it was.

When Zyair finally returned, Champagne blurted out, "Let's go to a strip club tonight."

Zyair hadn't even made it in his office good. "Did you say a strip club?"

The look on Zyair's face caused Champagne to laugh, "Why are you looking at me like that? We both said we would try new things. Well, let's start tonight." Champagne knew she wouldn't have to wait long for Zyair's response, because, being a man, this was one offer he couldn't pass up. She wasn't one to bad-mouth strip clubs. She just wondered why men frequented them. What was the point? After a couple of hours, didn't they get tired of seeing naked ass? Well, tonight she was going to find out what the hoopla was about.

"You want to go now?"

"Well, I was thinking we'd go home and change clothes first."

"Fine with me." Zyair couldn't get out the door fast enough.

On the way home, Champagne was tripping. She couldn't believe she was about to step in a strip club with Zyair. "What club are we going to go?" she asked him.

Zyair had to think about which one to take her to. He didn't know what would appeal to her. "It depends on what you're looking for."

"What do you mean by that?"

"Well, there are two types of strip clubs. You've got the ones in the hood, where any and everything goes and then—"

Champagne cut him off. "What do you mean, where any and everything goes?"

"Sex, drugs, and whatever else you can think of."

"What's the other type?"

"Upscale, hands off, more attractive. There are two kinds of strip clubs crunk/upscale. Believe it or not, most people have a better time at the crunk clubs as opposed to the upscale clubs because the dancers at the crunk club refuse to let a brother leave out the club with a nickel. They want all the money and they work for that money. Whereas, the other type of club, most of the women think that Spike Lee or some director is about to cast their asses."

"Champagne looked at Zyair. "How do you know so much?"

Zyair laughed. "I'm quoting Thomas."

That, Champagne could believe. "Why don't we go to both."

"Are you sure?" Zyair was still in disbelief.

"I'm more than sure. We can stay maybe an hour or two at one, then go see another."

Zyair was feeling like the man. "Your wish is my command."

He couldn't believe any of this was happening. He was actually going to the strip club with his lady. He felt a little weird about it, knowing it wasn't going to be the same as if he was with his boys.

Then again, maybe it was a good thing, because then Champagne would see that when he's with Thomas and the crew, he's not the wild, off-the-chain guy that gropes on, proposes, and gets oral sex from a stripper.

He hoped Champagne wasn't trying to set him up,

see how he was going to be if they did this threesome thing. Maybe he needed to stop thinking about it so much.

They were definitely trying to take their relationship to the next level. Zyair wondered how he should act. Should he act calm and not look around? He definitely didn't want to appear uptight in any way. When he was with his boys, they just entered the club, found seats, and started passing out singles.

Zyair didn't feel like second-guessing his actions, so he told Champagne while they were getting dressed, "I have to be honest. I'm a little nervous about this."

"What are you nervous about?"

"I don't know what to expect. I don't know what's acceptable and what's not. Do I tip? Do I just sit there? Do we call people over?"

"How about this . . . why don't we just go with the flow. Do what you normally do, and if I approve, I just might let you get a lap dance."

Zyair looked at her like, *Yeah right*.

Once in the car, they decided to go to Bottoms Up first. Zyair had never been there, but he'd heard a lot about it. He'd heard that the dancers were shapely and that for most of them anything goes. Heck, a man can hope, and his hopes were high.

Champagne glanced over at Zyair and wondered what he was thinking. If she wasn't mistaken, he had a little smirk on his face. She could just imagine. She had to admit, she was a little nervous as well. What if she got there and was disgusted? Then again, what if she got there, was turned on and lost her damn mind.

She pulled out her lipstick case; touched up her lips. Her heart was racing, but she was determined to see this through. After all, it was her idea.

Zyair decided to start from the bottom and work his way up. He couldn't wait to hear what her opinion would be of the spots.

When they pulled into Bottoms Up parking lot, Zyair looked at Champagne. "Are you ready?"

She opened the door and replied, "As ready as I'll ever be."

When they entered the club, Champagne felt like she was on the set of a BET afterhours video. Not only were women walking around with nothing on, but people were everywhere. She had to walk through a crowd and say excuse me numerous times just to get to where she was going.

Looking around, Champagne was surprised to see that there was an even number of men and women there. She told Zyair, "Damn, it's crowded as hell in here."

Zyair noticed as they walked through, men and women checking Champagne out. They paid no attention to him.

Some guy had the audacity to come up to Champagne and ask her, "What time are you dancing?"

Zyair looked at him and said, "She's not."

The dude looked Zyair up and down, decided he didn't want any trouble, and just walked away.

Zyair asked her, "Do you want to stay here?"

"I'm okay. Let's just stick together."

Zyair had no intentions on letting Champagne out of his sight. If she had to go to the bathroom, he was going with her. If he had to go, she would be with him.

After squeezing their way through the crowd, Zyair spotted an empty corner of a couch. He took Champagne's hand and pulled her towards it.

The second they sat down a young lady dressed in

the smallest and tightest dress either of them had ever seen asked them if they wanted a drink.

Champagne ordered an apple martini, and Zyair ordered a Corona. Before their drinks arrived two women came over to them and asked them if they wanted a table dance or to go into the VIP room.

Champagne looked them both up and down. They were total opposites, one was real short with at least size D titties. Champagne wondered how she got those big-ass breasts on that little body. Her hips were small, and her breasts were the only curves she had, average in the face, with "weave of life." Champagne knew she would not be the one.

The other girl was a little cuter, but a bit too thick, borderline chubby. She also had the weave of life.

What's up with all this fake-ass hair? Champagne didn't' really know what her type was, but it definitely wasn't these two.

Zyair was watching Champagne, waiting to see how she would answer them.

"No, thank you."

They looked over at Zyair.

"You heard the lady."

When the girls left, Champagne wanted to know what happens in the VIP room.

"Every and anything," Zyair informed her.

When the drinks were brought over, they sat back on the couch, sipped and watched the dancers.

Champagne couldn't believe all that she was seeing. If she wasn't mistaken one of the dancers appeared to be pregnant. Men were putting their hands inside women's panties, that is if they were wearing them. The women were bending over, opening their pussies up wide. It was a hot mess.

"See anybody you want to tip?" Zyair asked.

There actually was one girl that had gotten Champagne's attention. Champagne heard someone call her Chocolate.

That she was. Chocolate-complexioned, medium height, probably about five-four, size C breasts, a small waist, and an ass for days. When she turned around, Champagne noticed the butterfly tattoo on her ass, a wing on each cheek. When she made her booty clap, the butterfly appeared to be flying.

Before Champagne could get a chance to call her over, someone else did.

"You want a lap dance?" Champagne asked Zyair.

Before he could give her an answer, Champagne calls someone over and tells her, "Give my man a lap dance."

Zyair looked at Champagne and asked her was she sure.

"Yes, I'm sure. I might get one after you."

That was something Zyair couldn't wait to see. "Maybe you should go first."

"No, you go first."

The next thing you know, it was on. Zyair was sitting straight up, real tight. He kept telling himself, "Don't get hard. Don't make it seem like you are enjoying it too much."

Champagne could tell what he was trying or more like trying not to do, so she grabbed his hands and told him, "Loosen up. We're here to have fun. You have my permission." She placed his hands on the dancer's breasts.

Champagne them summoned over another dancer and told her she wanted a lap dance as well.

Zyair was in complete shock. He was too focused on

what was going on with Champagne to really get into his own lap dance.

Champagne was allowing this woman full access to her body. Her hands were everywhere. It wasn't until the girl tried to expose Champagne's breasts that she put an end to it.

Zyair was a little relieved because although turned on, for a second there he was getting a little jealous.

When the dancers walked away, Zyair saw Champagne look up at Chocolate, the girl with the butterfly on her ass.

Champagne pointed her out to Zyair. "I think she's sexy."

Little did she know, Zyair already noticed that Champagne had been peeping her.

The girl saw Champagne point her out and started coming in their direction.

On her way over to them, she was grabbed by another girl, who was just as sexy.

Zyair glanced at Champagne and thought to himself, *It's about to go down.*

They both stood in front of Champagne, all eyes on her.

"I saw you watching me."

"I was," Champagne admitted.

"I'm Chocolate. This is my girl, Cinnamon. You want a private show?"

Zyair wanted to yell out, "Hell yeah!"

"What does a private show entail?" Champagne asked, pleased that Zyair was letting her take the lead.

Zyair wasn't crazy. He knew what he was doing. He knew to let everything be Champagne's idea.

"Well, you can get a private lap dance, you and your man, or just you and he can watch. For one hundred dollars, you can watch us do each other, and for a hundred dollars apiece we'd do you both."

Zyair didn't open his mouth. His eyes said it all, "Just say yes to anything."

Before Chocolate could continue on with her proposition, there was a ruckus two tables over. Two men were arguing. Champagne couldn't make out what they were saying, but she could make out that one of the dudes had a gun.

Zyair spotted it the second she did. He grabbed her hand, pulled her up, and along with others, they ran out the club.

After making it to the car, Champagne and Zyair looked at one another and burst out laughing.

"Can you believe that?" Champagne asked. "We could have gotten killed while trying to get our freak on."

Zyair started the car up. "Where to next? Do you want to go home, or do you want to try the other place?"

"What's it called?"

"Fantasies."

"Is that where you and Thomas go?"

"I've never been, but I heard it was upscale and that the quality of women is definitely of a higher class."

"How much higher in class could they be if they're stripping?"

Zyair didn't have an answer.

"Let's go. I'm not ready to turn in yet." Champagne had to admit, she wanted to see more. She was also glad things happened the way they did, because she wasn't sure what answer she was going to give the Chocolate girl, but she knew it was a yes to something.

When they arrived at Fantasies, Champagne noticed

the difference immediately. One, it cost twenty dollars per person to enter, two, the clientele was predominantly white businessmen. The dancers were more attractive and had better bodies than the other women at Bottoms Up.

Another major difference was that someone seated you and gave you a menu with the prices of all the services they provided.

Although the atmosphere was more appealing, the prices were ridiculous when you compared them to Bottoms Up.

"Goddamn!" Champagne stated.

The same girly show that they could have witnessed at Bottoms Up for fifty dollars would cost them one fifty here, and the only thing that a single was good for was a peek at someone's titties. And a drink was ten dollars, with a two-drink minimum.

After being seated, they decided to at least get a lap dance, which was twenty dollars. After all, they'd paid their money to get in.

Champagne picked out a Spanish girl who called herself Shala. She promptly ran down the rules of the lap dance. By the time she was done with the rules, Champagne said exactly what Zyair was thinking, "Let's leave."

When they got to the car, Zyair asked Champagne what would she like to do now.

"Go home," Champagne said, ready to make love.

Zyair broke the speed limit all the way home. What would have normally been a forty-five-minute drive took thirty minutes.

Neither of them said a word. They just headed towards the bedroom.

When they stepped in, Champagne asked Zyair,

"When I was getting my lap dance, did you like watching?"

"I always like watching." Zyair was referring to the strip club and Jamaica.

Champagne started to undress, and Zyair knew this meant for him to do the same.

In less than five minutes, Zyair was kneeling between Champagne's knees, his face deep in her pussy, and his hands on her breasts, squeezing her nipples. Champagne threw her head back and told him, "Lick it, lick my walls."

Zyair separated her lips to put his tongue in as far as he could. He pressed his chin on the lower part of her pussy and shoved his tongue in and out of her like it was a dick.

Champagne held his head tight against her and humped his tongue. "Suck my clit," she demanded. She was ready for an orgasm.

And Zyair was ready to give it to her. He was also ready to get deep inside her. This was his pussy, and he wanted her to know it. He wanted to hear her say it. He took both of his hands and pushed the skin back from her clitoris and flicked his tongue back and forth, then suckled it, flicked back and forth and suckled some more.

He knew she was about to explode when her body started quivering and bucking.

"Oh, Zyair, it's yours, baby," Champagne called out as she climaxed.

Zyair removed his mouth and climbed on top of her. He gripped both cheeks of her ass and entered her real patient-like. He wanted to feel every inch of that pussy, and he wanted her to feel every inch of him.

He pulled out on a one, two, three count and slammed inside her. It was driving them both crazy.

It wasn't long before Zyair looked Champagne in the eyes and said, "I'm about to come," and come he did. Hard.

CHAPTER FOURTEEN
"MY GIRL"
TEMPTATIONS

The next day Zyair, floating on cloud nine, met Thomas at the gym.

Thomas was spotting Zyair and could tell something was up. "All right, out with it."

"Out with what."

"What's got you so happy this morning?"

"You wouldn't believe me if I told you."

"Try me."

"Let me finish up these chest presses, then I'll tell you."

Thomas couldn't wait, so he refused to spot Zyair until he spit out whatever information he was about to share.

Zyair sat up on the bench, shook his head and said, "Man, you'll never believe what Champagne and I did this week?"

"What?"

"Went to a strip club."

"Together?"

"Yep."

Thomas stood in front of Zyair. "You're straight lying."

Zyair lay back down on the bench. "Why would I lie about a thing like that?"

Thomas took the bar and placed it in Zyair's hand. "Because, man, I thought she hated you going to strip clubs."

"She hates me going with *your* ass."

Zyaid did a few press-ups, placed the weight back on the bar, sat down and said, "Guess what else?"

Thomas raised his eyebrows. "I don't know if I can take anything else."

Zyair needed to tell someone of their adventure for the weekend and there was no one he really trusted with issues of the heart other than Thomas. Patting his chest, like "I'm the man," he told Thomas, "She suggested it. She also let me get a lap dance."

Thomas took a step back, looked at Zyair and told him, "You're lying," but the look on Zyair's face told him he was telling the truth. "You're one lucky man."

"Don't I know it."

"What's gotten into you two? First you go to Hedonism, then you go to the strip club together. What's next? Swinging?"

Zyair stood up. "Hell no!" He grabbed his towel and his bottled water off the floor. Together they headed towards the locker room.

Thomas couldn't let the conversation go. "Never say what you won't do because to me it seems like you two are on your way to a whole other level of freakiness."

Zyair just laughed. He knew Thomas wanted to hear more, and there was only so much information he was willing to give up. "Man, come on, let's go get something to eat."

* * *

In the meantime, Champagne was in her office. She had another interview set up today and Lord knows she hoped this one prospective employee was better than the others. She really needed to hire an assistant and fast. There were a couple of events coming up for her clients and her being the sole everything to everyone wasn't working. Nor was her being picky.

Zyair had told her, "That's how it is sometimes, and it's better to be picky and take your time than to hire someone just because you're in a hurry. When you have your own business and you're doing all the hiring, you have a hard time choosing someone because your company is your business, your baby, and you don't know who to trust or who will take it as seriously as you."

She'd set up this interview downstairs in the café like she did the others.

Please let this be the one, please let this be the one, she thought over and over to herself. She needed to do business without having to worry about if something was going to get done or not.

Champagne told the person she was interviewing that she would be sitting at the table in the corner, closest to the kitchen. That way they wouldn't be looking around for one another.

After glancing at her watch, Champagne decided to leave fifteen minutes early and have a cup of coffee or tea so that she would be relaxed by the time the young lady arrived. She grabbed the folder with the resume in it, locked her office door and headed downstairs. When she got to the door, she looked at where they would be sitting and saw someone already there. She headed towards the table.

The young lady seated there stood up. "Champagne?"

"Candy?"

"Yes." She put out her hand for Champagne to shake it.

Champagne felt a sense of relief. Candy was professionally dressed. She wore a black pants suit with a white tailored blouse, opened-toed heels, small silver hoop earrings, and had her hair pulled back. She was attractive in a don't-have-to-try-hard kind of way. Champagne was also impressed with the fact that she'd arrived early and wasn't chewing gum.

"I apologize if my being early is an inconvenience, but I figure it's better to be early than rushing or late."

Champagne sat down and told her, "That's okay." She placed the folder with Candy's resume on the table. She waved her hands for Candy to sit as well.

Champagne sat back and crossed her legs, "So, tell me about yourself. Why do you want this position?"

Candy went on to tell her she'd always been interested in the entertainment business and after being a personal assistant for an executive at a law firm, she grew tired of the corporate world and made the decision to leave and look for something where she could combine her skills and something she loves.

"When I saw the position for this job in the paper, I decided to give it a try and send in my resume."

Champagne went on to ask her a number of questions about her past job and about her organizational skills.

At the end of the interview, Champagne didn't bother having her fill out the personality test. She knew she'd found the person.

"If I was to hire you, when would you be able to start?"

"I could start as soon as tomorrow."

Champagne stood up to signal that the interview was over.

Standing up, Candy asked her, "How soon before you make a decision?"

"In the next day or two. I'll give you a call either way."

They shook hands and went their separate ways.

When Champagne got back to her office, she called Alexis and told her, "Girl, I think I've finally found an assistant."

"Good for you, girl."

Champagne could tell that Alexis was pre-occupied. "What are you doing?"

"Nothing. Laying here with Khalil."

Champagne rolled her yes. "Why don't y'all come over for dinner?"

"When? Tonight?"

"How about tomorrow?"

"Hold on."

Champagne heard Alexis ask Khalil if he would mind going over Champagne's for dinner the next day. She couldn't hear his reply.

"We'll be there," Alexis told her. "What time?"

Off the top of her head, Champagne told her to be there by eight p.m.

They hung up the phone. Champagne called Zyair and told him about Candy and dinner.

Feeling good about the day, Champagne thought, *Why wait? I already know I'm going to hire her.* So she picked up the phone and called Candy.

"Hello?"

"Candy, this is Champagne."

"Oh, hi."

"I'm calling to say you've got the job. Can you come

by the office Monday around one p.m., so we can talk more about what's required?"

"Sure, I can do that."

"Okay, I'll see you then."

"That you will."

Champagne hung up, pleased with herself. She found an employee, and she was going to give Khalil the opportunity to impress her.

CHAPTER FIFTEEN
"SUPERFREAK"
RICK JAMES

That evening while relaxing on the couch, with her legs thrown over Zyair's and her eyes closed, she laid her head and recalled the night of the strip club. She had to admit that she had a good-ass time and was even thinking about going back.

She wished she could tell Alexis about it but knew this was something she had to keep to herself. Alexis wouldn't understand at all. When she really gave it some thought it pissed her off because she wanted a best friend that she could share any and everything with.

When Champagne opened her eyes, Zyair was looking at her.

"What were you thinking about?"

"Nothing. I was relaxing."

"Nah, I could hear your mind working. Come on, give it up."

"You really want to know?"

"I wouldn't have asked if I didn't want to know."

"Okay." She sat up. "I was thinking about the strip club."

This got Zyair's attention. "Oh really?"

"I came up with another idea."

"Oh really?" he repeated.

"Let's go to a gay club."

"What?" Zyair stood up. "I don't know about all that."

Champagne started laughing.

"What's so funny?"

"Do you think I'm talking about a men's club?"

"If you're not, then what are you talking about?"

"An all-girls club."

Zyair sat back down. This was something he had to think about. Champagne seemed to be pressing this girl-girl issue. First she wanted to see some naked ass. Now she wanted to see women dancing with women.

On the one hand Zyair was excited about the turn of events, but on the other, he couldn't help but think about all the horror stories he'd heard about men "coming out" and leaving their significant others.

Deep down in the back of his mind, he was a little apprehensive about going to the gay club. What if Champagne saw some girl, fell in love and left him. *Nonsense*, he thought to himself. *Champagne likes dick too much*. Plus, he knew he could throw down in the bedroom.

Nonetheless, Zyair was so nervous about agreeing to yet another adventure that he decided he would come up with some "gay-club rules." Rule number one was Champagne must stay in Zyair's sight at all times, rule number two was Champagne must stay in Zyair's sight at all times, and rule number three was Champagne must stay in Zyair's sight at all times.

"Okay," he told her, "let's go."

"Cool."

"But I've got three rules," he told her.

"What kind of rules could you possibly have."

He told her the three rules, and her reply was a kiss and an, "I love you too."

"Are you nervous?" Zyair asked Champagne as they got dressed.

"A little," Champagne confessed.

"I am too."

"Yeah, right. Your ass is probably excited."

"I'm not going to lie, I am excited, but at the same time, I don't know what's going and what's not going to happen."

"Well," Champagne said, "what do you want to happen?"

"It's up to you."

Champagne looked in the mirror, she was wearing a pair of Seven Jeans and a fitted black tee with black stiletto shoes. She was going for the casual yet sexy look. "How do I look?"

Zyair, who wore jeans and a black T-shirt, told her, "Sexy."

It was just what she wanted to hear. "Okay, let's go."

After searching on the internet, they'd chosen a club in the city.

When they arrived in the city, Champagne suggested driving past the club so they could see the clientele. "Just to get a feel of it first," she told him.

Zyair knew that was part of the reason, but he also knew the other part was to get her nerves up before entering.

The windows were dark, and the door was closed. Sitting on the outside of the door was a white female with a spiked haircut stamping people's hands as they went inside.

Damn, the stereotype is true, Champagne thought.

"So is that your type?" Zyair joked.

Champagne didn't know if she had a type when it came to women. What she did know is that if she was to deal with one, she had to be very feminine, similar to herself.

They drove around the block one more time before looking for a parking garage.

As they walked towards the club, Zyair asked Champagne, "Are you ready?"

She took a deep breath. "I'm ready if you are."

"ID please," the girl at the door said.

Damn, this chick is bigger than me, Zyair thought to himself. It definitely wasn't the same girl that was sitting on the stoop when they initially drove by.

They pulled out their IDs and handed it to her.

She took a quick glance at Zyair and a lingering look at Champagne, looking her up and down. She even had the audacity to lick her lips and say, "Hope you find what you're looking for."

Neither of them answered her. They stepped into the club and looked around. On entry level of the club there was a bar the length of the floor. All the seats at the bar were taken. There was also a pool table in the back of the room, and house music blared through the speakers.

"Let's walk around," Champagne suggested. As they walked around, Champagne noticed that there was no particular type in the club. The women didn't all look like men or dress like men, they didn't all have short haircuts, and they definitely weren't of one race. There were also as many men as there were women in attendance. She wondered if they were experimenting just like she and Zyair.

Women were hugged up on one another, holding

hands and kissing. She even saw some women approaching others, and it bugged her out that it was done in the same fashion as a man would approach a woman. Even some of the same lines were used.

"Yo, what's up? I haven't seen you here before."

"Do you want to sit at the bar, or do you want to go upstairs and dance?" Zyair could hear the house music playing and knew Champagne loved that type of sound to dance to.

"Let's just chill down here for a little while," Champagne said. When Zyair didn't respond, she looked up at him, only to find him staring at something to the right.

Her eyes followed his gaze and landed on two women in the corner kissing and embracing passionately. They appeared to be lost in one another. Against her will, Champagne found her pussy tingling. She was full of nervous energy and could feel every nerve in her body.

She and Zyair must have been staring real hard because when the women came up for air, they both looked their way and smiled, causing them to look away in embarrassment.

"Maybe we should go upstairs," Champagne suggested. Dancing would relax her. When they reached the top of the stairs, Champagne located the bar and grabbed Zyair's hand. "I need a drink to loosen up."

He followed her while looking around. Eventually they found a table in the corner and sat down.

As they order a drink, a woman approaches Zyair. "Do you mind if I dance with your friend?"

She was quite attractive and reminded Champagne of Victoria Rowell from *The Young and the Restless*, a sexy, innocent look.

Zyair looked at Champagne, who nodded.

What the heck. Might as well make an adventure of it, she thought.

Not wanting to seem overly possessive, it took everything in Zyair's power not to get up and follow them to the dance floor, but after about three songs and what seemed like twenty minutes later, he stood up to see what the hell was going on.

Before Zyair could spot Champagne, she appeared in front of him with a totally different girl.

"Zyair, this is Selena. Selena, this is my husband, Zyair."

Zyair was pleased Champagne introduced him as her husband because he was feeling somewhat left out and lonely and wanted some attention.

"Come dance with us," Selena said.

Zyair stood up and followed behind them. He couldn't help but notice that Selena had an ass like Deelishis from *Flavor of Love*.

Champagne stood in the middle of them as they danced.

Zyair would tell Selena things like, "Grab Champagne's ass. Kiss her on the neck. Rub against her titties."

It must have been the liquor because Selena's hands were all over Champagne.

Aw shit, this might be it, Champagne thought. *We really might be able to set this up*. Champagne gave Zyair a look to try convey what she was thinking, but that thought went out the window the second Selena pulled out a cigarette.

"I'm going to have a smoke," she told them. "Care to join me?"

Reading one another's mind, they both said no.

The rest of the night was uneventful. Champagne

danced a couple more dances, and Zyair drank a few more drinks.

Champagne noticed that Zyair may have had one too many drinks. "Baby, I think we should leave."

Zyair knew she was right. He also knew that he would not be the one driving home, that Champagne would.

As they walked towards the door, Champagne could feel someone staring at her. She turned around and saw that it was Candy, the girl she'd hired.

Damn! Should I speak?

Before she could make that decision, Candy turned away.

Relieved, Champagne told Zyair, "Wait near the door. "I'll get the car."

Zyair slept all the way home.

Champagne went to bed a little agitated because she wanted sex and Zyair was in no shape to give it to her.

CHAPTER SIXTEEN
"FAKE"
ALEXANDER O'NEAL

Champagne chose not to spend the weekend focusing on the fact that she saw Candy at the club. She knew she would have to decide whether she should address the issue or leave it alone. Today wasn't the day to make that decision. She needed to clean the house and prepare dinner for Zyair and their company. How she would get through this day with the hangover she had, she still didn't know, but hope was alive and if she finished it early, she'd be able to lay down before the guests arrived.

As a matter of fact, she was going to have to lay down if she wanted to be a gracious host. The reason she extended the invitation was because she wanted to get to know this Khalil character a little better. After all, he was spending a lot of time with her best friend.

Earlier that day, Zyair was on the phone and mentioned the dinner get-together to Thomas.

"Is Alexis bringing that new nigga?"

Zyair didn't recall telling him. "How do you know she's with someone?"

"I saw your girl and she told me."

"Oh."

"Well, is she bringing him?"

"Yeah."

"Well, I'm coming too."

"No, you're not."

"Why not?

"Because I know you. You've got a thing for Alexis, and I can see you starting some shit."

"Man, please, I won't bust his ass. I just want to see the knucklehead. Plus, ain't nothing like a home-cooked meal."

"I don't know, man. I don't think Champagne is going to like this."

Just then, Champagne walked into the kitchen. "You don't think I'm going to like what?"

Zyair didn't answer. He handed the phone to Champagne.

"Hello?"

"What's up, beautiful?"

"Quit brown-nosing and tell me what I'm not going to like."

Thomas, never one to bite his tongue, said, "I want to come over for dinner."

Normally, Champagne would have thought about it, but this time, she didn't. They could both evaluate this Khalil character. "Okay, just don't come empty-handed. Bring some wine or something." She passed the phone back to Zyair, who was staring at her in disbelief.

She turned around to finish cooking. "What?"

When Zyair and Thomas finished talking, Zyair walked into the kitchen and stood in front of Champagne, his arms crossed. "Okay, out with it."

"Out with what?"

"You're up to something. I can feel it."

Champagne tried to walk around him, but he kept blocking her path.

"I don't know what you're talking about."

Zyair placed his hands on her hips and held her in place. "Don't start any trouble."

Champagne kissed him on the lips. "I'm not."

Zyair released her, not believing a word she said.

"Is he coming by himself, or is he bringing someone?"

"He's bringing someone."

"Okay."

That afternoon Champagne was able to take a nap. When she woke up, she noticed Zyair had fixed the table and cleaned the kitchen.

"Thanks, sweetie," she told him.

"You're welcome."

A couple of hours later, they found themselves dressed and sitting in the living room watching television. Champagne heard someone pull into the driveway. She walked over to the window, opened the blinds and saw a Quicksilver Cadillac EXT. She watched as Khalil got out of the driver's side and went around to open the door for Alexis, who had a box in her hand. She quickly closed the blinds and opened the door.

She greeted Alexis with a hug and said hello to Khalil. She could see why Alexis was attracted to him. He was definitely good-looking in a thuggish sort of way. He stood over six feet, his goatee trimmed to perfection, and you could see his muscular build through his designer gear. He was a chocolate pretty boy.

Before she could close the door, another car pulled into the driveway. Thomas climbed out of his black CLK 350 and noticed everyone standing in the doorway, looking his way. He glanced at the EXT and then at Khalil.

The young lady he was with was still sitting in the car. "Are you going to open the door?" she asked him.

He walked over and let her out, as Alexis and Khalil went into the house and Champagne waited at the door.

Champagne hugged him and pulled away. "Thomas, who's your date?"

By now Zyair was at the door, looking at Champagne out of the corner of his eye.

"This is Diamond."

Champagne noticed that Diamond was stunning. "Hi, Diamond. Come on in."

Once everyone was in the same room together, introductions were made, and Champagne took the box from Alexis.

"It's dessert."

"Oh shit," Thomas said, "I left the wine in the car. I'll be right back."

Zyair followed Champagne in the kitchen. "You need to tell me what's going on."

"Nothing. Why do you keep asking me that?"

"Because I know you."

Champagne started laughing. "Stop worrying so much. Let's just enjoy the evening with our friends and their dates."

When they walked back into the living room, Diamond was asking Khalil if she knew him from somewhere.

"No, I don't think so."

"You just look so familiar to me."

"Well, you know what they say, we all have a twin."

Thomas was looking Khalil up and down. It was so obvious that Zyair bumped up against him.

"What?" Thomas asked.

"Let me show you something."

Thomas wasn't stupid. He knew Zyair was trying to get him out the room to lecture him.

"Nah, man, show me later."

"Come on, everyone, let's have a seat and get to know one another." Champagne pointed towards the seating area.

For the next hour, conversation flowed back and forth freely. They learned that Khalil was one of the partners for a construction company and that he grew up in Atlanta and moved to New Jersey to help one of his sisters, who was having problems with her husband, and ended up staying.

Champagne noticed that Diamond kept staring at Khalil like she knew something no one else did.

Thomas stood up to go into the kitchen to get some ice, and less than a second later, Champagne walked in behind him.

"So what do you think of this Khalil guy?" she asked him.

"I don't know. It's something about him I don't like."

That was just what Champagne wanted to hear. "I feel the same way."

They exchanged a look. They both knew that a more in-depth discussion had to take place later.

Dinner proceeded in an uneventful manner, and surprisingly everyone got along fine. Champagne still felt suspicious about Khalil and couldn't get past the instant dislike she felt for him. She had to admit to herself that she played it off pretty well.

When the time came for the party to end, Champagne said, "We should do this again."

They all agreed, and Zyair and Champagne walked everyone to the door.

Alexis asked Champagne, "What are you doing tomorrow?"

"One of my clients have a book signing."

"Oh, okay. Then call me when you get a chance."

CHAPTER SEVENTEEN
"I DIDN'T MEAN TO TURN YOU ON"
CHERELLE

Champagne stood next to her client, Hunter Irby, whose self-help book, *Lovin' the Skin You're In*, was on numerous bestsellers list. She noticed that Hunter was fading fast. This was the second signing that day, and they were both tired and hungry.

Champagne leaned over and whispered in Hunter's ear, "It's almost over. Put a little more pep in your step and then it's a wrap."

Hunter looked at her and plastered a smile on her face in readiness for the next reader.

This was part of Champagne's job, keeping the clients on their toes, making sure they presented themselves in the best light possible. Champagne didn't attend every event with her clients. There wasn't enough time, but sometimes she liked to show them how important and valuable they were to her. Soon she would be attending events even less, once she was able to hire a couple of more people.

After two hours of shmoozing at this book signing, Champagne just wanted to go home and relax.

Hunter was getting out of her seat so they could pack up and leave, when a woman came running over. "Wait, wait," she said.

Champagne looked up. "You've got one more," she told Hunter.

Hunter already had the book signed when the lady reached the table. Her pen poised for the name, she asked, "Who do I make it out to?"

"Sharon Simmons."

Upon hearing the name, Hunter looked up and started laughing. She stood up and reached out to give Sharon a hug. "Oh my God, what are you doing here?"

"I heard you were doing a signing and had to come see you."

Champagne took Sharon in with her eyes. She didn't know what had gotten into her. She was checking women out a little too often now and was hoping it wasn't noticeable.

Facing Champagne, Hunter introduced them to one another. "Sharon's a childhood friend of mine."

Extending her hand out for a handshake, Champagne said, "Pleased to meet you."

Sharon started laughing. "Girl, I don't shake hands. I hug." She placed her arms around Champagne and pulled her close, adding a little squeeze. "So what are you ladies about to do?"

Champagne shrugged.

Hunter looked at Champagne. "Well, let's go to dinner," she volunteered. "My treat."

Champagne's plan was to go home and cook dinner, but there was something about this female's energy that she was feeling. She found herself wanting to know a little bit more about her. "Now, you know I'm not one to turn down a free meal,"

"I know a nice spot. It's about twenty minutes from here. A friend of mine owns it. Is that too far?"

"What kind of friend?" Hunter asked.

Sharon laughed and winked.

Champagne wished she was in on the joke.

"Let me give you ladies the directions, and we'll meet there," Sharon told them.

Twenty minutes later they stepped into the restaurant. Sharon asked the hostess to get the owner.

"May I ask your name?"

"Tell her it's Sharon."

Less than five minutes later, the owner appeared. "Sharon," she greeted her, and they kissed on the lips.

Champagne noticed the owner's hands were almost touching Sharon's ass and that she'd also closed her eyes when they kissed.

"Hunter, Champagne, this is Barbara."

Everyone said hello.

"Follow me," Barbara told them as she led them to a booth that seemed to be hidden away in the corner.

Once they were seated, Barbara told them she would send someone over to take their order. As she walked away she said, "Sharon, don't leave without saying good-bye."

"Oh, I definitely won't."

Over the course of dinner, Champagne learned that Sharon was gay, not bisexual, that she liked women only. She wondered if she was "her type." *Stop it. Stop thinking these thoughts.* It was thoughts like this that made her question herself. What if she was really gay and just in denial? Nah, that's not it. This was just a moment, a phase she was going through.

When dinner ended and they were walking to the car, Sharon pulled out a business card and handed it to Champagne. "It was a pleasure meeting you. Call me sometime."

Champagne told her, "I enjoyed meeting you too. I'll definitely give you a call." She gave Sharon her card and placed Sharon's card in her purse. She noticed Hunter watching them with an amused look on her face. Thank God, she didn't ask any questions.

"We'll be in touch," Hunter told Champagne when Sharon drove off.

"That, we will."

When Champagne arrived home, Zyair wasn't home, so she called Alexis up. There was no answer, so she did the next best thing and went to bed. The day had been exhausting, and it was a rare moment when she got to turn in early.

Monday finally arrived. Zyair and Champagne were standing in the kitchen, Champagne making an espresso and Zyair peeling open the eggs he'd just boiled.

Zyair knew Champagne had something on her mind. She'd been quieter than usual that morning. After slicing the eggs, he asked her, "What's on your mind?"

"Huh?" Champagne pretended she didn't hear him.

"Where's your head at? You seem lost in thought this morning."

She wasn't lost in thought, she was thinking about Sharon and wondering when and if she should call her. If she did, what would they talk about? Would they go out to lunch? Would she be the female she slept with? Of course, she wasn't going to tell Zyair any of this.

"I'm just trying to organize the day's activities in my head."

"What do you have planned?"

"My new person is starting today."

"That's exciting."

Champagne didn't find it exciting. If anything, her nerves were shot.

Once Champagne arrived at the office, she was relieved that she'd told Candy to arrive at one p.m., as opposed to nine a.m. Now she had a chance to think about how she would handle Candy seeing her and Zyair at the club. Maybe she should just act like it wasn't anything. Sometimes the best thing is to do nothing at all.

Shaking her head, Champagne decided not to focus on that. What she needed to do was put together a list of duties that need to be completed by the end of the week. So far, Champagne had nine clients. Their professions ranged from writer to company CEO.

Each client needed something different, whether it was booking interviews, making flight arrangements, putting their calendar together, making sure they showed up when they were supposed to, and on and on it went. She definitely needed someone to start right now. Four employees including herself would be ideal, but right now she'd settle for three—herself, Candy, and another.

The pickings were limited. Nobody she'd interviewed to date had what it took. Champagne was considering hiring an intern from college or someone straight out of college. The more she thought about it, the more it seemed like a good idea. If she did that, she would be able to mold the person. Initially, she'd wanted someone with experience, but she realized that it sometimes came with attitude.

After making several phone calls, typing up a to-do list and, working on her companies website, Champagne glanced at the clock. She couldn't believe it was twelve already. Only one hour left before Candy showed up. Maybe less because, during the interview, she'd mentioned being a stickler for time.

Champagne needed a break and decided to run downstairs to the café and grab a salad and something to drink.

Over the past couple of weeks, before going upstairs to her office, she'd made it a habit to grab a cup of tea and the newspaper. The owner of the café always spoke to her, and today was no exception.

Champagne was waiting on her salad when the owner walked over. She couldn't remember his name for the life of her.

"So how's business going?" he asked.

"It's going. I'm having a hard time finding another employee."

"What kind of position is it?"

"Administration, and assisting me."

"I just might know someone."

Champagne couldn't hold it in any longer. She had to tell him she forgot his name.

"That's okay. It's James."

"James, in case you forgot, I'm Champagne."

"I haven't forgotten."

Champagne could hear the flirt in his voice. As long as he didn't try to come on to her, it was all good. "So who is this person you have in mind?"

"My niece. She just moved here from Virginia, and she's looking for a job."

"What kind of experience does she have?"

"I'm not sure, but she's smart and can type. I'm not just telling you that either. After all, you know where I work."

Champagne laughed. "Call her. I'll be more than willing to meet with her. I'll bring a card down later."

The girl behind the counter gave Champagne her order, and Champagne paid for it and went upstairs.

She glanced at the clock and saw that she was downstairs for twenty minutes. "Damn." She only had fifteen or so minutes to eat.

Champagne sat at her desk and ate a portion of her salad, still wondering once again what she was going to do about Candy seeing them. She was almost certain Candy wouldn't bring it up.

It was five to one when Candy knocked on Champagne's open office door. "Hello."

Champagne was startled. She was in the middle of filing and didn't hear Candy walk in. "Hey, how are you?"

"Excited about my first day."

Pulling the chair out from behind her desk, Champagne sat down and told Candy to have a seat. Before she could even sit down, she said, "On second thought, let's sit at the table. That way I can go over a few things with you."

Looking at Candy, Champagne knew that she wouldn't be able to move forward without bringing up and moving past the fact that they'd seen one another over the weekend. Crossing her arms and leaning back in the chair, Champagne cleared her throat. "There's something we need to discuss before we move on to my expectations."

Candy had an idea what she was talking about. Of course, she wasn't going to bring it up, but she was glad Champagne did. She was curious to know whether her boss was gay and who she was with. Was it her husband, a friend, a brother, a lover?

Candy was well aware of the fact that a lot of couples frequented gay clubs to add spice to their relationships. As a matter of fact, she'd taken part in a couple of these escapades. Is that what Champagne's outing was about?

"This weekend we saw one another out, and I want you to know that what's done outside of this office, on personal time, is just that—personal. If seeing me out is going to affect how we work together, you need to let me know right now."

Champagne chose her words carefully. The more she'd thought about it, the more she felt it unnecessary to justify or explain why she had been at Fantasies. It was her and Zyair's business, not anyone else's.

Damn, that's all she's going to say. "No, of course not. We're both adults, and it is what it is."

"Good." Champagne uncrossed her arms and slid the folder across the table. "Inside are some forms that need to be filled out. Once you're through with them, we'll go over your job description and what's expected."

Candy took the folder, opened it, and pulled a pen out of her purse.

Champagne stood up. "I'll be in my office. Let me know when you're done."

In less than fifteen minutes Candy knocked on the door. "I'm done."

For the next half an hour, Champagne filled Candy in on her expectations. She told her that over the next two weeks, she would be responsible for answering the telephone, taking detailed messages, and going through the files and learning about the clients, amongst other things.

Candy was anxious to get started. The only part of the job description she wasn't feeling was the answering-the-phone part. She didn't take this job to be a receptionist.

Just as she was thinking it, Champagne told her, "You won't be answering the phone for long. I'm looking to hire another person."

Together they determined for the time being that Candy would work from twelve to five p.m. Champagne did explain to her that in this line of work she had to be flexible and that some evenings and some Saturdays were required.

"Don't worry, you'll know in advance when you're needed, and we'll work something out as far as the normal hours go," Champagne reassured her. She also gave Candy a tour of the office. "Until I hire someone, you'll sit up front. Hopefully, that won't be for long, then the office to the right is yours."

Candy looked to the right. *Damn, my own office space.* She was liking that.

By the time they finished talking and going over how Champagne liked things done, it was four p.m. Champagne was worn out from talking. "You can leave early today."

"Thanks." Candy put up the papers she was looking over and told Champagne she would see her tomorrow.

When Candy left the office, Champagne breathed a sigh of relief. It felt good to finally have someone else in the office. It made it feel like a real business and not a one-person show. She knew that running her own business was going to be a challenge, but she just didn't realize how much of a challenge it would be.

Champagne was starving. She never got a chance to finish her salad. *I bet you it's soggy now. I know I should have had them put the dressing on the side.*

She reached for the phone to call Zyair. The second her hand touched it, it rang. She pressed the speakerphone button. "Personal Touch, how may I help you?"

"Um, hello?" the voice on the other end said.

Champagne picked up the phone and placed it between her ear and shoulder. "Hello?"

"May I speak with Champagne?"

"This is she."

"Hey, lady, it's Sharon."

Champagne was pleased to hear her voice. "Hey."

"Do you remember me?"

"Of course, I do. How are you?"

"Fine. I was sitting here in my office and came across your card. Since I hadn't heard from you, I thought I'd give you a call."

"Well, I'm glad you did."

Champagne held the phone up to her ear and started pacing the floor, feeling a little nervous, as if she was on the phone speaking with a man. Champagne recalled being attracted to her and had even thought about her a number of times. She just couldn't bring herself to call her.

"Are you up for dinner this evening?"

Champagne wanted to say yes right off the bat, but she knew she should call Zyair first to see if he had anything planned. She didn't feel like going through the process, so she said, "I'm free tomorrow."

"I'm not for dinner, but I am for lunch. Is that good for you?

It would only be Candy's second day. Champagne wasn't sure if she wanted to leave her alone in the office so soon. Then again, she was a grown-ass woman, and it was only lunch. "Yes."

"Good. Listen, I've got to go, but I'm looking forward to seeing you tomorrow. We'll meet downtown at Cora's Kitchen. You know the place?"

Champagne told her, "I do. They have the best soul food in the area. What time?"

They agreed on one p.m. and hung up.

Champagne sat back in her chair, placed her hands in her lap, and closed her eyes. She pictured Sharon and the way sexiness oozed from her body. What if she'd seen her at Fantasies? Would they have danced together? Would she have taken her home?

Champagne wondered what they'd discuss at lunch. Would they have idle chitchat? Would they talk about one another's sexuality? *I could always bring it up in the conversation.* The more Champagne thought about it the more she was like, *It's time to get the ball rolling. If I'm going to sleep with another woman, I need to go ahead and do it, instead of thinking about it.*

On that note, Champagne decided to call Zyair and see what he was up to, how his day was going. She was ready to broach the subject again.

CHAPTER EIGHTEEN
"I WANNA SEX YOU UP"
COLOR ME BADD

Zyair wasn't in his office to answer Champagne's phone call. He'd been to the bank.

The second he entered his office, DaNeen followed behind him. "I don't mean to bother you, but there's something I need to talk to you about."

"Give me about fifteen minutes to get settled and then I'm all ears." Zyair didn't like being rushed. He needed a few minutes to get it together.

DaNeen wanted to talk now. "Fifteen minutes?" She'd been putting off resigning for quite some time. Now she was ready to let him know that she'd be moving on. She was going to start her own dessert business and was going to ask him to be her mentor.

"Yes. Then I'm all yours."

DaNeen stood there and looked at him like she wished he was all hers. "You promise?"

Zyair didn't answer her. He just smiled and watched her as she walked away. After all, he wasn't stupid. He knew that she was attracted to him, and he to her. He also knew not to act on that attraction. Anyway, it would only lead to heartbreak and death. Champagne would kill him.

Zyair thought about the time DaNeen decided she wanted to come onto him. Of course, he turned her down. Now if he wasn't with Champagne, he might have took her up on her offer. She had sexiness oozing off her. That was one of the reasons he'd hired her. He recalled when she came in for her interview. All the other women he'd interviewed came dressed in too extremes, either casual, everyday, "I'm-going-to-chill-with-my-girls" outfits, or over-the-edge "I'm-going-to-a-club" outfits. He didn't know what they were thinking. His restaurant was upscale, so he wanted someone that represented that in speech and appearance. He was at the point of disgust, thinking he'd never find the right person. If push came to shove, he'd do hosting duties himself until he found the right person.

When DaNeen had walked in, he almost jumped up and hugged her. He wanted to hire her on the spot but knew that wouldn't be wise. Looks didn't mean a thing if you couldn't deal with people.

Eyeing her from head to toe, he took in her pencil-thin skirt that hugged her curves and fell just above her knees. Her top was crisp white, tucked in at the waist and grazed her breast. She didn't have on stockings, which didn't bother him because her open-toed shoes showed perfect feet. Her hair was natural and buzzed cut, and she had diamond studs in her ears. It appeared as if the only makeup she had on was lipstick and eyeliner. He'd noticed it all in an instant and was taken. *This is a natural beauty,* he thought.

As he interviewed her, he found her to be intelligent, funny, and sassy. For a minute there, he wasn't sure if he should hire her because he was attracted to her, but he was desperate. His other hostess had to resign because of a family emergency. Hire her, he did, and he'd been pleased with his decision ever since.

Zyair noticed he'd left his cell phone on his desk. He clicked down to missed calls and saw that Champagne had called. He tried calling her back, but it went straight to voicemail. "Hey, sweetie, just returning your call." He then retrieved his messages from his service. *I'll return phone calls later.*

Picking up the phone, Zyair paged the front desk. "Send DaNeen in please."

Less than a minute later, she was walking into his office.

"Close the door," he told her.

She did.

"Have a seat."

When she sat down, Zyair couldn't help but notice the slit in her skirt revealed a lot of her toned thighs. The skirt definitely hugged every curve.

"What can I do for you?"

DaNeen crossed her hands and placed them in her lap. "I'm leaving," she blurted out.

Zyair frowned. He didn't understand what she was talking about. "Leaving? Where are you going?"

"I'm resigning. I've decided to start my own dessert business."

"Wow! Where did that come from?"

Zyair didn't know she baked, didn't know she wanted to start her own business. Hell, when he thought about it, he didn't know a lot about her.

"It's something I've always wanted to do. As a matter of fact, when you hired me, I recall mentioning to you that I bake."

"I know you did, but that's not the same as saying, 'I want to bake for a living.'"

"At the time, it was just a dream. Between working here, watching how you run your business, and taking entrepreneur workshops, I've realized it's something I could do as a business."

"Do you have any potential clients?"

"Well, I've been baking for parties and weddings. I also have two mom-and-pop restaurants I bake for."

"Impressive."

"You see, my working here has taken up so much of my time. I could use that time to get clients, you know, target restaurants."

"How come you never approached me about stocking your desserts?"

"I don't know. I just didn't."

"The first lesson you need to learn about business is to take advantage of every opportunity."

As DaNeen stood up, Zyair noticed her curves once again. *I wonder if she would be down for a threesome.*

"The other thing is, I need a mentor and I wanted to know if you would be it."

Without a second thought, he told her, "Sure."

DaNeen came around the desk and threw her arms around him, kissing him on the cheek.

At that exact moment, Thomas came busting through the door. "Yo, man, you wouldn't"—He stopped midsentence and wondered what the hell was going on. "Oh, excuse me, I didn't mean to interrupt anything."

DaNeen stepped back. "I'm sorry," she told Zyair. "I just got carried away."

Thomas was taking it all in with a raised eyebrow. He sat down and followed Zyair with his eyes as he stood up to walk DaNeen to the door.

"Listen," Zyair told her, "you don't have to quit. We can work something out until you're up and running."

From where Thomas was sitting, it appeared as if DaNeen batted her eyes and pushed up her cleavage as she said, "Are you sure? I don't want to be an inconvenience or anything."

"I'm sure," Zyair reassured her, and closed the door behind her.

Thomas couldn't wait for her to leave the room. "What's up with you and her?"

"Nothing, man. She's my employee."

"Are you sure she's not more than that?"

Zyair didn't bother answering the question. He just sat down behind his desk. "What's up?"

Thomas started to speak, "Listen, the—"

"Wait, before you even tell me. What I tell you about busting in my office without knocking?"

"I see why you feel that way now."

"Man . . . please. You know I'm as loyal as they come."

Thomas stood up. "Remember at dinner, my girl kept saying she knew that Khalil dude from somewhere?"

"Yeah."

"Well, you're not going to believe this shit."

The way Thomas was acting, Zyair could tell it was something big. "What?"

"That niggah is a freak. Listen to this—he fuckin' hangs out at that club, Free for All."

Zyair had no idea what he was talking about. "Free for All?"

"You know, the swingers club?"

"How does your girl know?"

"She's a freak too!"

Zyair laughed.

Thomas wasn't done yet. "Not only that, but he's done porn too." Before Zyair could get a word in, Thomas added, "She's bringing me the tape tonight. You know we've got to tell Aexis, right."

Zyair started shaking his head. "Nah, man, that's something I'm not getting into."

"What do you mean, you're not getting into it. We're talking about my future wife, and your woman's best friend."

"And?"

"Do you care about Alexis?"

"Man, don't ask me no stupid shit like that. She's my girl's best friend. Of course, I care about her."

"Do you care about your boy?"

Zyair just looked at him.

"Well, I love that girl."

"Yeah, okay."

"I'm going to marry her one day. As soon as I get all this fucking around out of me, she's going to be mine. I don't want this Khalil character to ruin her."

"She's a grown-ass woman."

"I know that, but I think you should at least tell Champagne."

"I'll think about it."

"Nah, man, action. We need some action."

"I told you I'll think about it."

"I don't want him destroying my goods."

"I heard you, man."

Thomas stood up. On his way to the door, he turned around. "Be careful."

"Of what?" Zyair had no idea what he was talking about.

"That fine honey you got working for you."

Zyair waved the comment off. "What is this, first grade? I'm a taken man."

Thomas wasn't fooled. He knew Zyair was bothered because what he'd said was true. Thomas looked at him real serious and said, "Yeah, and you need to remember that shit."

CHAPTER NINETEEN
"TEMPORARY LOVE THING"
FULL FORCE

Champagne was nervous as she got ready for lunch with Sharon. Was it just lunch, or would it be considered a date?

Maybe it was because she was going to lunch with a lesbian, or maybe it was the fact that she figured that Candy was either gay or bisexual.

Champagne had noticed how appealing Candy was when she'd interviewed her. And today, for some reason, she kept sneaking peeks. She knew if she didn't hurry up and handle this threesome thing with Zyair she was going to go crazy. It was consuming her. Maybe once they did it, it would be out of her system.

"I'll be back in two hours," Champagne told her after she'd given her a list of things to do and a few phone calls to make.

"If I have any questions, should I call your cell phone?"

"That would be fine."

Fifteen minutes later, Champagne was entering the restaurant. The second she put her foot through the door, she and Sharon spotted one another at the same time. Champagne could feel Sharon checking her out as she walked across the room. She found herself looking down at her outfit, hoping Sharon liked what she saw.

When Champagne reached the table, Sharon surprised her by standing up, walking around the table, and kissing her on the cheek.

"Thanks for coming," she said.

"No need to thank me. I wanted to."

Sharon licked her lips. "Did you now?"

Champagne caught it and figured it was just something she did when talking, that it wasn't a signal or a sign.

At that moment the waitress walked over and placed menus on the table. "Would you ladies like something to drink?"

Sharon looked at Champagne.

"Diet coke, please."

"I'll take the same." The second the waitress walked away, Sharon said, "So tell me about yourself."

"What do you want to know?"

"Let's start with why you said yes to my invitation."

"I found you interesting," Champagne told her.

"Interesting how?"

All of a sudden Champagne felt shy, but she wasn't going to let that get in her way.

"Maybe *interesting* is the wrong word. What I mean is, you know how you meet someone and you like their vibe immediately . . . when you feel like, that's a person you can kick it with?"

"Yeah, I know."

"Well, that's why I agreed. That and the fact that Hunter thinks you're cool as hell."

"The feeling is mutual. Hunter and I have known each other for ages."

I wonder if they were lovers.

"Do you want to know why I called you?" Sharon asked, breaking Champagne out of her thoughts.

"Because you think I'm cool as hell?"

"Cool, cute, and sexy."

The waitress came with their drinks. "Are you ready to order?"

They told her they needed another minute.

Champagne and Sharon quickly picked up their menus and started looking at the choices.

"I think I'll order the salmon dish," Champagne said.

"Yeah, that's a good idea. Plus, it's light." Sharon waved the waitress over and placed their order.

While she did that, Champagne decided to continue flirting with Sharon. Why sit here and pretend? She was on a mission. When the waitress walked away, Champagne said, "So you were saying?"

"I was saying that I think you're cute."

"Cute's for kids."

"How about, I think you're sexy as hell?"

"How do you know I won't get offended? How do you know if I'm even attracted to women?"

"I don't know. If you're offended, please tell me."

"I'm not."

"Good. Because when we met, I thought I was feeling an energy."

Champagne frowned. Was she that obvious? "What kind of energy?"

"And I'm checking you out on the 'quiet-tip' energy."

Champagne laughed. She did think it was on the quiet tip. "Damn!"

"Let me ask you this," Sharon said. "What's your sexual preference?"

"Confused."

Sharon leaned across the table, surprised that Champagne gave her such an honest answer. "Confused?"

Champagne spotted the waitress heading their way with their plates. She waited until she placed them down and walked away. Then she told Sharon, "Listen, I want to be clear, honest, and upfront."

"Damn, girl, I didn't know this lunch date was going to be this serious."

"I didn't either, but I've got a feeling about you."

"What kind of feeling?"

As they ate and talked, Champagne talked about the Hedonism experience she and Zyair had. She hadn't told anyone else about it, and it felt so good to get it out.

"Ever since that experience, I've been thinking about doing it again. I want to see if I'll enjoy it as much sober, or if it was just a drunken experiment."

"What do you want it to be?"

"I'm not sure. I mean, what if I enjoy it the second time around and can't get enough? What if I get turned out?"

"How are you going about looking for this female? Don't tell me you and your man went to a strip bar or a gay club."

Champagne started laughing. "Why not?"

"You have, haven't you?"

"Yep."

Sharon just shook her head. "Don't you know that's what all couples do when they're trying to get it on? Why do they think it'll be that easy?"

"Believe me, we know it's not."

"Why don't you two use someone you know?"

"We don't know anyone that will be down."

"What exactly are you looking to make happen?"

Champagne couldn't help but wonder, Was Sharon asking all these questions because she might be open to it, or was she just asking out of curiosity?

"Well, Zyair can look, maybe touch. I'm not even sure about that."

"What else can he do?"

"What do you mean, what else can he do?"

"Is he going to be involved sexually?"

"As in intercourse?"

"What else?"

"No, this is really about me."

Sharon sat back in her seat. "What if I told you I was interested?"

Champagne sat back in her seat too. *Shit, she's just playing with me.* "I thought you didn't like men?"

"I never said that. I don't have anything against men, I just don't want one in my bed. Plus, you said he'd just watch."

Champagne felt her pussy get instantly wet. Could this really be happening? Had she actually found the person? What would Zyair say? What would he think of Sharon? After all, she is fine. Would he be attracted to her, not that it would matter, because she wouldn't be attracted to him.

"I don't know what to say."

Sharon reached across the table and took Champagne's hand. "Don't answer that right now. Go home, talk to Zyair about it. Let me know what he says."

Liking her touch, Champagne asked, "Why are you offering to be the one?"

"Because you look like you'll taste good."

There was nothing Champagne could say to that comment. She was sure Sharon could feel her hands sweating.

"Let's enjoy the rest of our meal," Sharon said.

All Champagne could do was agree.

On the way back to the office, Champagne imagined she and Sharon making love, Sharon's hands and mouth all over her body. She thought about Zyair sitting across the room or on the foot of the bed watching as Sharon played with her titties and licked her juices. She pictured him masturbating while watching.

Champagne knew her thoughts were racing out of control when she almost ran a red light. How she made it back to her office in one piece was a mystery to her.

Candy was sitting at the receptionist's desk, and on the telephone when Champagne walked in. In the sitting area on the couch sat a young lady reading a magazine.

"Hello," Champagne said.

"Please hold," Candy said to whomever she was speaking to on the telephone. She looked up at Champagne. "This is a potential client."

Champagne glanced at the young lady on the couch.

"Hi, I'm Shay," she said as she stood up. "I was down at my uncle's, and he told me you were looking to hire someone. I thought I'd drop my resume off."

The last thing Champagne felt like doing was speaking on the phone or interviewing someone. She needed to get her head together after the conversation she and Sharon just had. She also wanted to call Zyair, but she didn't want to be rude. She told Candy to take a very detailed message.

Champagne walked over to the desk and reached past Candy. "Excuse me." She couldn't help noticing how good she smelled. She pulled open a drawer and pulled out a piece of paper and gave it to Candy. "As a matter of fact, ask them these questions and tell them I will get back to them."

She looked at Shay and told her, "Give me five minutes and I'll speak with you."

"Thank you," Shay answered.

Champagne went into her office, closed the door behind her, and exhaled. She sat at her desk to clear her head and tried to focus on the business at hand.

Five minutes later, she opened her door and told Shay, "Come on in."

Champagne could see the nervousness on her face. "No need to be nervous. This isn't an official interview."

That didn't turn out to be true, because thirty minutes later, Shay was walking out the door with the job. "Thank you. Thank you so much," she told her as she was leaving.

Champagne smiled. She felt in her heart that she'd made the right call hiring this young lady. There was something about her, that "it" thing people talked about. She'd moved here on her own with money saved, found an apartment, and up until this moment was working various temp jobs.

After she was gone, Candy knocked on Champagne's door.

"Come in."

"So did you hire her?" Candy sure hoped so. She couldn't wait to do hands-on work, get involved with the stars, party plan, do the fun and exciting part of the job.

"I sure did. She's starting tomorrow."

"That's good."

Champagne told Candy to have a seat, and they

talked about how her first day on the job went, if it was what she expected.

Champagne then told her that she was going to let her assist with planning a party for an up-and-coming actress.

Now that's what I'm talking about, Candy thought.

As Champagne stood up to leave, Candy stopped her, "Champagne?"

"Yes?"

"I just want to thank you again for this opportunity. I promise, I won't let you down."

Champagne nodded. "I know you won't."

"See you tomorrow," Candy told her.

"That you will."

CHAPTER TWENTY
"BACK AND FORTH"
CAMEO

Over the next couple of days, Champagne kept wondering how she was going to tell Zyair she thought she'd found the one. The reason she had yet to tell him was because at first she thought maybe she'd do a "we just happened to run into one another, and oh, by the way, this is Sharon" routine. That idea came and went because she didn't think she'd be able to pull it off.

"Did you tell him about me yet?" Sharon asked, when they spoke earlier that day.

"No, not yet."

"Are you chickening out?"

"No."

"Aren't you ready for my tongue?"

Whenever they talked, Sharon was always messing with her this way, saying things to turn her on. *Verbal foreplay* is what she called it.

"I'm ready. I'm going to do it today."

* * *

Zyair had told her earlier that he would be home early and hinted that he'd love some of her home cooking. "I've missed you," he told her. "We haven't been spending enough time together since you started your business."

"You knew it was going to be that way."

"I know, and I'm not complaining. I want to you to be as successful as you want to be. I just need some time with my lady."

The way Champagne decided to play it was to cook his favorite, yet simple meal of meatloaf, mashed potatoes, and broccoli. Then they'd make love, and when it was over, she'd bring up Sharon. She'd say something like, "I've befriended this girl."

Of course he'd ask who, and she'd tell him she was a gay girl. From there the tale would unfold.

Too bad that's not the way it went. The second Zyair entered the house, she knew it wouldn't wait past dinner. She was too hyped. "I found her," she blurted out.

"Found who?" Zyair had no idea what Champagne was talking about, but he could tell from her body language that she was excited about it.

He followed her into the kitchen, where she started to pour them each some wine.

"What are you talking about? Who have you found?"

Champagne handed Zyair the drink. "You know . . . her."

Still a little confused, Zyair looked at Champagne, who started to move her eyebrows up and down.

"Oh, her?"

"Yes, her."

"Who is she? Where'd you find her? How did you

meet her? Did she approach you, or did you approach her?" He had a ton of questions for Champagne.

Champagne told him how she and Sharon met. She told him about them going out to lunch and having a few casual conversations. "The next thing you know, she was telling me she was gay."

"So, she just came out of nowhere and told you that?"

Champagne wasn't sure how much she wanted to tell him and how much she wanted to leave out. "Well, I was talking about you and the fact that you own one of the top restaurants in the area, and she said her ex-girlfriend owns a restaurant."

Zyair really hoped this wasn't someone he knew."

"Which restaurant?"

When Champagne told him, he felt a little relieved that he didn't know her personally. Of course, being in the business he'd heard of her. "Go on."

As Champagne went on with her story, Zyair had to admit to himself that he was feeling somewhat left out, the same way he felt at Fantasies. He thought they'd find someone together. He didn't think she'd initiate it on her own. However, the thought of another woman in his bed outweighed any minor fear.

"How did you ask her?"

"I didn't really ask. She sort of volunteered."

Oh hell no.

Zyair wasn't stupid. That meant this chick was trying to get with Champagne anyway. She must have wanted her real bad to suggest it. He needed to know all the details before he made a decision.

"How did she volunteer?"

"We were talking about relationships and sex."

"Sex?"

"Women talk about sex all the time. She was telling

me about Hedonism. She asked me if I'd been there. I told her what happened with us while we were there, and she asked me if I ever thought about doing it again. So I told her yes."

Zyair wasn't too sure if he really wanted to go through with it again. Plus, it sounded a bit too coincidental. Between going to the strip club and the gay bar, he was feeling like Champagne wanted this just a tad bit too much. He didn't tell her he was having second thoughts, though, and decided to just go along with it and hope that it didn't blow up in his face.

That night as they lay in bed, Zyair suggested to Champagne that they watch a porno movie, something they hadn't done in quite some time. Probably since they first got together.

"Why? I don't think we should watch one. We need to just go with the flow."

He didn't want to press her. He thought to himself. *I'll just watch in the morning when she goes to work.*

That night when they made love, Zyair was trying to go all out, over-caressing, over-kissing, and basically overdoing it.

"Sweetie, this is not a competition," Champagne told him. She could tell he was trying to prove a point.

She could also tell that his excitement about the whole thing was wearing thin, so she decided to bring their lovemaking up a notch. While he was inside her, she closed her eyes, pressed him down inside her, and started to grind her hips in a circle, knowing he wouldn't last too long.

And he didn't.

Afterwards as Champagne slept, Zyair had a difficult time falling asleep. In his gut, he felt concerned. Not wanting to feel like an outsider in his own house, in his own bed, he was telling himself he had to be in control of the situation at all times. What happened if this girl started giving it to his woman better than he could? How would he handle that? He didn't think about any of that when they were in Hedonism because that was a spur-of-the-moment situation. This one, however, was going to be planned.

He wondered what this Sharon girl would be open to. Would she let him touch her? Would she suck his dick, or was she one of those lesbians that would only let him watch? *Shit, was there levels of lesbianism?* he wondered.

Then there was the fact that she was a lesbian, and not a woman into men *and* women. Did that mean all he could do is touch? Would he even be allowed that much access? He wanted to join in, at least get his dick sucked by her.

It's official. He'd bitten off more than he could chew. It was time to come up with some rules for real. Rules such as, anything sexual will only occur when both of us are present. He wasn't crazy. He'd heard stories about how people started sneaking off and seeing one another. Another rule, there'd be no "being the best of girlfriends." Hell nah, that wasn't happening. He was going to have to figure out how to handle that one because they were already talking on the phone and having lunch together.

Zyair felt Champagne stir. He shifted a little closer to her, hoping to wake her.

"Why are you still up?" she asked, interrupting his thoughts.

"I don't know."

Champagne didn't believe that. After all, she was right next to him and was feeling his energy and his restlessness. "Do you not want to do this? Have you changed your mind?"

Not wanting to change his mind and outright disappoint her, he needed to think on it for one more day. "No, I haven't changed my mind. I'm just a little disappointed that you went about this without me. I feel left out. After all, this was suppose to be an 'us' thing, not a 'you' thing."

Champagne didn't say a word. She knew what he was saying was true.

"What if I came home and said, 'I found her,' to you?"

Champagne answered honestly, "I wouldn't like it."

"I know you wouldn't."

They both remained silent for a minute.

"You know what," Zyair said, "I'm bugging, that's all. Let's go ahead and do this."

Champagne sat up. "I don't want you to do something you really don't want to do."

Zyair was ready to end this conversation. "I want to. Let's go to sleep and talk about it in the morning."

"All right." Champagne laid back down and cuddled up next to Zyair, her back to his chest. Then she turned around and kissed him on the lips. "I love you."

"I love you too," Zyair told her.

The next morning when they awakened, neither brought up what they'd talked about the night before. Zyair had made up his mind that he was going to let it happen, and once it's done, that was going to be the end of it.

Champagne was ready for it to happen and wanted to ask him, "When?" but she decided to wait and speak with Sharon first.

CHAPTER TWENTY-ONE
"I WONDER IF I TAKE YOU HOME"
LISA LISA

Alexis sat in Champagne's office with some serious news to share with her girl. As she waited on her to finish talking to the receptionist, she was growing impatient.

"I'm sorry," Champagne said when she entered the office and closed the door behind her. "It's been a hectic day."

That morning when Champagne arrived, both Shay and Candy were there. Champagne gave Candy a list of things to do. One of her actress clients was starting a foundation and some research needed to be done. If Candy did a good job, Champagne would consider letting her come with her out of town to meet the client.

Alexis stood up and gave Champagne a hug. "Girl, I've missed you."

They hadn't talked or seen one another since they had dinner at Champagne's.

"I missed you too," Champagne replied. "Between me and my business and you and your man, we haven't had the time to see one another."

When Alexis thrust her right hand out and started wiggling her fingers, Champagne couldn't help but notice a ring. "What is that?"

Alexis could barely contain herself. "I'm engaged, girl."

Champagne plopped down in her chair.

"Did you hear me? I'm engaged."

Champagne thought Alexis had lost her mind or declared temporary insanity. "Engaged?"

Alexis could tell that Champagne wasn't happy about the news. "Aren't you happy for me?"

There was no way on God's green earth that Champagne would even pretend she was happy. If that made her a bad person, so be it. There was something about Khalil that rubbed her the wrong way, and she was going to find out what it was.

"You just met him."

"I knew you were going to say that. I know we haven't been seeing each other that long, but you can't help who you fall in love with."

Champagne wanted to throw up. She couldn't believe Alexis was talking about being in love and she barely knew the man.

"In love? Girl, please . . ."

Alexis sat back in her chair and crossed her arms. "I don't even feel like sharing my good news with you. I come in here all excited, wanting to tell you about my engagement, thinking you'd be happy for me and support me, but no, you don't even congratulate me."

Damn, she sure knows how to make a girl feel bad. "I apologize, Alexis. If you're happy, I'm happy."

Alexis pouted. "You don't mean it."

Champagne stood up, walked over to Alexis, grabbed her hands, and looked her in the eyes. "I love you, girl, and I am happy for you. I'm just concerned and scared. What if—"

"Let's not do the what-ifs." Alexis pulled her hands away. "I could 'what if' my relationship to death. Hell, I could 'what if' our friendship, I could 'what if' life, and it'll get me nowhere."

Champagne threw up her hands. "Okay, you're right. I'm being an ass. I apologize. Let's start over." Champagne pulled Alexis out the chair.

Alexis frowned. "What are you doing?"

"We're starting over. Go to the door and act like you just walked in."

"Are you serious?"

"Come on, please." Champagne wanted to make it right.

Alexis decided to play along. She stood up and walked to the door.

"Go ahead."

Alexis came running towards her. "Oh, girl, guess what?"

"What?"

Alexis stuck her hand in Champagne's face and wiggled her fingers. "I'm engaged."

Champagne threw her arms around Alexis. "I'm so happy for you. Let me see the ring again."

Knowing they sounded phony as hell, they both started laughing, and Alexis thanked Champagne for trying.

Alexis sat down and turned serious. "Listen, I know you love me and that you worry."

"I also think you deserve the best God has to offer."

"How do you know it's not Khalil?"

Champagne felt like rolling her eyes but didn't want to hurt Alexis's feelings again. "You know what, you're right. I don't know. He just may be the one intended for you."

Alexis gave Champagne a hug, stood up, and started walking towards the door.

"Where are you going?" Champagne asked. "You just got here."

"I love you, girl, but I've got to run. I just wanted to stop by and share my news with you."

Champagne told Alexis she loved her too and walked her to the door. The second she got back into her office, Champagne picked up the phone to call Zyair, but he wasn't available.

She needed to speak to someone about this engagement and the only other person she knew that would care was Thomas. *Damn! Think, Champagne, what's his number?*

Champagne closed her eyes to try and recall the numbers on the caller ID at the house. *Five, five, five, four, two, no, no, that's not it. Five, five, five, six, nine, eight.*

Snapping her fingers, she opened her eyes and dialed a number. Thomas picked up the phone.

Champagne didn't even say hello. "Can you believe he asked her to marry him?"

"Who the hell is this?" Thomas yelled into the phone.

"It's me, Champagne."

"Oh. What's up?"

"Alexis got engaged to that Khalil guy."

"Repeat what you just said."

"I said Alexis got engaged to that Khalil dude."

"What the hell are you talking about? You didn't tell her?"

"Tell her what?"

"About the porno and the swingers club."

"Thomas, I don't know what you're talking about. What porno, and what does it have to do with Alexis?"

"I told Zyair."

"Will you tell me what the hell you're talking about." Talking in circles was getting on Champagne's last nerve.

"The young lady I was with at your dinner party, remember she kept saying she thought she knew him from somewhere?"

"Yeah."

"Well, it turns out she knows him from this swingers club she goes to occasionally, and on top of that he used to be a porn star."

Champagne almost dropped the phone. "You told Zyair about this?"

"I told him to tell you."

"You know what, let me call you back." Champagne went to hang up the phone, but she heard Thomas yell in the background, "Wait!"

"What?"

"Are you going to tell her?"

"You're damn right, I am."

"Let me ask you this, Would you want to know without proof? And before you say yes, think about it. You know how you women are. You have to see it to believe it or have hard evidence."

"Shit, shit, shit, shit!" She hated that he was right. "So what are we going to do?"

"We're going to get evidence. My girl thought she had the movie he was in, but she doesn't. I'll try to locate it, and in the meantime, we can go to the swingers club."

Champagne pulled the phone away from her ear. "I know you're crazy. There is no way in hell I'm going to one of those places with you."

Thomas laughed.

"What the hell is so funny?"

"Girl, please . . . I'm not trying to have Zyair kill me.

What I was thinking about is casing the joint, maybe even setting him up."

"How are we going to do that?"

"Diamond will help us."

"Are you sure?"

"I'm sure."

"Okay, then set something up with her. Call me and let me know what and I'll do whatever I have to do, short of going inside the swingers place."

"Cool."

"Thomas?"

"Yes?"

"Diamond was your date, right? Why would she help you?"

"Don't worry about that. She and I are good friends. Plus, she owes me one."

After hanging up, Champagne picked up the phone to call Zyair again. Before she could dial the number, there was a knock on the door.

"Come in."

It was Candy, "Didn't you say you wanted to meet with me today?"

"Yes, give me about twenty minutes. Bring with you the research information you did."

"Okay."

Champagne was unable to reach Zyair. *What the hell is he up to? Is he that busy that he couldn't call me today?* She was pissed off at him and needed him to know it. How dare he have information about Khalil and not share it with her? She could hear him now, "It's not our place, and it's not our business."

That's some bullshit. Her best friend is her business.

CHAPTER TWENTY-TWO
"MY PREROGATIVE"
BOBBY BROWN

"Why haven't you answered my phone calls?" Champagne asked Zyair when she was finally able to reach him. "I've been trying to call you all day."

"Remember I told you I have a couple of meetings today? You know I'm trying to get financial backers."

Champagne forgot all about it. She'd been so consumed with herself. She almost felt bad for not really listening to Zyair, but not so bad that she'd hold back her wrath. "How come you didn't tell me what Thomas told you about Khalil?"

"I didn't know whether I should or not."

"You didn't know?"

"That's what I said." Zyair wasn't digging the tone of Champagne's voice. He'd been dealing with assholes all day, begging for money, and to now be putting up with some bullshit wasn't going to fly with him. "Listen, I think you need to stay out of this whole Alexis-Khalil affair."

Champagne couldn't believe he would say that, knowing how close they were. "So, you're telling me if you knew something about one of the women Thomas was messing with you wouldn't say anything?"

"Listen," Zyair said, "I've had a long day, and I'm really not in the mood for a confrontation."

Before Champagne could answer him, Shay buzzed in.

"Hold on," Champagne told Zyair. "Who is it?'

"It's someone named Sharon."

Champagne picked up the line Zyair was on and told him she'd call him back, that a client was on the other line. Why she lied, she didn't know, especially since she could have called Sharon back.

As soon as Champagne came back on the line, Sharon said, "What's up, sexy?"

"You." Where that reply came from, Champagne had no idea.

"So did you tell your man about me?"

"I did."

"And?"

"Honestly, I think he's having mixed feelings."

"Mixed or jealous feelings?"

"Both."

"So what's the final verdict?"

"Here's what I was thinking. Why don't you stop by his restaurant for a drink this weekend? That way you two can meet, and we'll take it from here."

"I can do that."

They continued to make small talk and hung up about fifteen minutes later.

What are you doing? Champagne asked herself. She needed to just drop this whole thing, but she was like a woman possessed.

She didn't know if she should bring it up again when she arrived home. She didn't want Zyair to let his imagination run too wild and start thinking she was going to do this with or without him. A part of her was thinking about doing just that, but she didn't want to go behind his back. She preferred to be upfront about everything. She didn't like being secretive, and that's why she wanted to tell Alexis what she knew.

Champagne called into the intercom, "Candy!" She needed an outsider's opinion. "Come here please."

Ten seconds later, Candy was walking in the office. "Yes?"

"Let me ask you a question. If you knew that your friend's mate did some things in the past that were just foul and may potentially be doing them now, would you tell them?"

Candy didn't need to think about it at all. "What I would do is get hard-core evidence. Or I'd let the person know what I know, and that if they don't tell, I will. I'll give that person the room to come clean."

"Okay, thanks."

Candy stood waiting. "Is there anything else?"

"Nope. Nothing else."

Champagne hoped Thomas would hurry up and call her back. She didn't want to walk around carrying this burden, withholding important information from a friend.

In his office, Zyair was agitated, and all Champagne did was agitate him even more. How did she know what Thomas told him? There was only one way and that's Thomas's ass. Zyair picked up his phone and dialed the number.

The answering service came on.

"Call me. I want to know what you told Champagne and when you told her."

As he was hanging up the telephone, DaNeen poked her head in the office. "You have a minute?"

"I do," he told her.

She stepped in. "When do you think we'll be able to sit down and go over my business plan?"

"We can do it tonight," Zyair said, not in a rush to get home just to be told off.

"Are you sure? I don't want to put you out or anything."

"Nah, I'm sure. What's your schedule for today?"

"I get off at seven."

"Well, come by my office then."

DaNeen said, "Thank you," and walked away.

Zyair found himself following her with his eyes. *What am I doing?*

On the way home, Zyair shook off his attraction to DaNeen. He found himself having all sort of thoughts, a couple of them sexual.

Why? Why am I thinking about another woman when I've got a fine-ass woman at home? Maybe it's all these threesome discussions we've been having, and it doesn't help any that I watched that damn porno and one of the women reminded me of DaNeen.

One thing was certain. He didn't feel like having a discussion about Alexis, and all he wanted to do was make love before he went to bed.

Champagne was exhausted. The past couple of weeks were draining. She'd set up her office, got adjusted to her new environment, hired new employees, met a prospective lover, and found out her best friend was engaged to a man she couldn't stand and didn't know why.

She also entertained a couple of her former clients who stopped by, brought gifts, and expressed interest in becoming her client exclusively. They told her that they stayed with Jackson because of her. She just felt, though, that she needed to be careful and not take on too many clients. But, then again, what was "enough"?

Champagne walked through the front door of her house, dropped her briefcase near the couch, and went straight to the kitchen. She kicked off her shoes and went over to the cabinet for a wineglass, placed it on the counter and went to the refrigerator and took out her bottle of Moscato, an inexpensive, but smooth wine.

Zyair sometimes got on her about drinking cheap wine, but she just ignored him. She'd drink whatever she felt like drinking. After pouring a glass, she headed towards the living room. Suddenly, she turned around and grabbed the whole bottle.

Once in the living room, Champagne placed the bottle on the coffee table, stretched out on the chaise, and proceeded to sip her wine.

The next thing you know, she was being awakened by Zyair. "Hey, sleepy head." He kissed her on the forehead.

Champagne sat up and glanced at the time on the television. It read 1:32 a.m. "You're just now getting home?"

Zyair sat at the end of the chaise. "Yeah. I thought I would be home earlier, but two of my co-workers got into it in front of the customers and I had to intervene."

Champagne glanced at the empty bottle next to her. No wonder she fell out.

Zyair followed her gaze. "I see you had a party by yourself."

"I was trying to unwind," Champagne said, pulling herself up off the couch. She grabbed the bottle and her empty glass and headed towards the kitchen, Zyair following right behind her. She placed the bottle and glass on the counter.

Zyair didn't feel like walking on eggshells. "Do you want to talk about this Alexis thing? I don't want it to blow out of proportion, and you hold on to being upset with me."

"No. I have to make up my own mind about how I want to handle this."

Relieved, Zyair turned to walk away.

"But," Champagne started, turning him back around, "I am still upset that you knew about it and didn't tell me."

"Well, how did you know I knew anything?"

Champagne went on to tell him about Alexis coming to the office and announcing her engagement.

Even he was surprised and thought it was too soon for that.

"So I had to call Thomas to tell him."

Zyair wasn't buying it. "You called him because you knew he would react."

Champagne didn't deny it. This bothered Zyair. She wasn't one to call up his boys, and for her to call Thomas over something like this, he knew she was up to no good.

"Don't go destroying friendships behind this mess."

Champagne whined, "I'm not."

"I hope not." Zyair turned to walk away then stopped. "Are you getting ready to go to bed?" He placed his hand on the small of her back.

From the low tone of his voice and from the way he was looking at her, Champagne knew he was in the mood. All she was in the mood for was a quickie. Not wanting to let him down, she asked him, "Are you making me a proposition?"

"Of course."

"Well"—Champagne placed her hands on the front of his pants and grabbed his penis—"I have a proposition for you." She could feel him getting excited.

"Yeah?"

"Why don't we do it right here, right now? All I have to do is pull my skirt up and bend over. How'd you like that?" Champagne started to unbutton his pants.

"I thought maybe I could take a shower first."

"Well, I think you can take a shower afterwards. Come on, let's be spontaneous." She had his pants and underwear down, and Zyair stood at attention.

"Maybe that's not such a bad idea."

Champagne turned around, pulled up her wrinkled skirt, and pulled down her panties. "Do your thing, baby."

Zyair couldn't get into her fast enough. "How do you want it?"

"Fast and hard." Champagne started moving back into him.

Neither of them said a word, until Zyair exploded inside her. "Damn!" was all he could say as he pulled out.

CHAPTER TWENTY-THREE
"TURN OFF THE LIGHTS"
TEDDY PENDERGRASS

The following morning at the breakfast table, Champagne decided, *To hell with it.* She said to Zyair, "Can I call Sharon and have her come by tonight?"

"Why tonight?" *Why is she asking me this now*, he wondered. *Why did tonight have to be the night? Didn't I put it down in the bedroom last night?*

"Honestly?"

"Yes, honestly."

"I keep thinking about it, and I want to move past it. I think the only way to do that is to do it."

Zyair realized that this was something that wasn't going to go away. There was no way out, and he too was ready to end this chapter, so he agreed.

"Are you sure?"

Zyair felt like he really didn't have a choice in the matter, so he told her he was positive.

Later that afternoon, Champagne called Sharon and told her, "Tonight's the night."

"He said it was okay?"

"Yes."

"Are we meeting at your house?"

"Yes."

Champagne, are you sure about this? You think he's going to be able to handle it?"

"He handled it in Jamaica."

"Yeah, but this time is different. This time it's on the home front."

"I don't think he would have agreed to it if he couldn't handle it."

"All right, if you say so."

Champagne proceeded to give Sharon directions to her address, and the time she should arrive.

That day Champagne wasn't able to focus on anything at office. Her mind kept drifting, imagining what was going to happen. Thank God, it was Friday, because had it been any other day, her clients would have been shit out of luck.

The day couldn't go by fast enough, and when the time came for it to go down, Champagne and Zyair were walking around the house in total silence and anticipation. He was dressed comfortably in sweats and a T-shirt, and she had on a shirt-dress, with nothing underneath.

"How do you think it's going to start?" she asked him.

"I don't know," Zyair told her. "Let just let whatever happens happen naturally."

Champagne agreed. From that point on, she started watching the clock, waiting for Sharon to arrive.

From the time Sharon walked through the door, Zyair felt like a third wheel. Sharon came bearing gifts for Champagne, handing her flowers and candy.

Zyair thought Champagne was a little too happy,

and immediately became jealous. He offered Sharon a drink.

She declined then said, "Listen, we don't have to play the get-to-know-you game. We all know why I'm here. So where's the bedroom?"

Her aggressiveness threw Zyair off, but turned Champagne on. Zyair wondered, Should I follow them or wait until I was called?

He didn't have to wonder much longer because Champagne told him, "Come on."

Zyair was a little bothered by the whole thing. One, it was moving too fast, and two it was obvious he was just there to observe.

Champagne entered the room first. It seemed like it only took a couple of strides for Sharon to be standing in front of Champagne, and Zyair sat in the corner watching, taking it all in.

Sharon reached out and ran her hand down Champagne's face. "I want you."

Scared, Champagne could feel the nervousness in her stomach. She wondered, *How would the sex start? What would Zyair do while me and Sharon made love? Would he stay the whole time? Would he leave the room? How long would it last? Would Zyair want Sharon to leave immediately, or would she stay the night?*

Champagne glanced over at Zyair, who nodded his approval, silently telling her, "Get the show on the road."

Champagne led Sharon to the bed. *Should I stand? Should I sit?* She decided to stand and leaned in to kiss Sharon. She'd been wanting to kiss her since the day they'd met.

Sharon pulled back. "Let me kiss you."

Champagne relaxed and waited, and Sharon leaned in and softly placed her lips on Champagne's. Sharon pushed open her mouth and slowly ran her tongue in it. Her kiss was passionate and unrushed.

Champagne could feel her pussy throbbing. She wanted to grab Sharon's hand and press it against her pussy. Sharon must have been reading her mind because she told her, "Don't rush it."

Zyair sat back and let them do their thing. He released a tight breath. It was going to happen again, and this time, he was filled, not with anticipation, but with apprehension. He wanted to yell out, "All right, get going," but he knew that would ruin the mood.

Sharon led Champagne to the bed and slowly unbuttoned Champagne's shirt-dress. She was surprised to find that Champagne wore nothing underneath. "So you're ready for me?"

"Yes."

"Lay on the bed."

Zyair sat in the corner and admitted to himself, he was turned on. He wanted to take his dick out and play with it but decided to wait. He just let his hands drop to his side.

Champagne lay back on the bed, her dress open, and Sharon leaned over and ran one of her hands down her torso. "You're so toned."

When her hands reached Champagne's pussy, she cupped it and pressed the top of her palm down.

Champagne moaned and arched her back.

Sharon then leaned over Champagne and ran her tongue across Champagne's nipple so gently, it felt like a breeze. She did this repeatedly. Then she squeezed both breasts together and bit down.

This caused Champagne to jump. It hurt, yet it felt good.

Sharon, seeing Champagne's response, did this a few more times. Then she made her way down to Champagne's pussy.

Once between Champagne's legs, she played with her pussy lips, pulling on them with her hands and teeth.

Zyair stirred in his seat.

Sharon looked up at him and told him, "You can come closer," and he did.

Sharon sniffed Champagne's pussy. "I hope you taste as good as you smell." She placed two fingers in Champagne's pussy and opened and closed them. She did this with one hand, while squeezing Champagne's nipples with the other. "I'm about to eat this pussy raw," she said. Then she slid her fingers out real slow and stuck her tongue as far up in Champagne's pussy as it would go.

Zyair watched, intrigued. Sharon's tongue was so far up Champagne's pussy, even he was impressed.

Sharon started to move her tongue in circles, then made it pointy and tongue-fucked Champagne.

Champagne reached down and grabbed Sharon's head.

Sharon took this as a sign to move to Champagne's clitoris. She didn't have to go searching for it because it was in her face, hard and ready to be sucked.

While Sharon sucked, licked, and nibbled on Champagne's clitoris, Zyair had his hands in his pants stroking his dick.

It wasn't long before Champagne called out, "Oh shit, I'm about come."

Sharon wasn't ready for her to come yet. She wanted this to last a little while longer, so she removed her mouth.

Champagne tried to pop up, but Sharon pushed her back down.

"What are you doing?" Champagne asked.

Not answering her, Sharon placed one finger, then two, then three inside Champagne. Then she pulled them out and placed them in her mouth, sucking on them one at a time.

That shit turned Zyair on so much that he had to stroke his dick harder and faster than he wanted to.

"You like that?" Sharon asked Champagne. "Do you want to taste it?"

She dipped her fingers back in, pulled them out, and placed them in Champagne's mouth.

Tasting her own juices made Champagne want to taste Sharon's, but before she could say anything, Sharon replaced her fingers with her mouth once again. This time it was obvious that she was ready to make Champagne explode.

Champagne closed her eyes and started grinding her hips against Sharon's mouth.

All the while, Zyair was playing with his dick. He wasn't doing it to come. He was going to save that for Champagne.

Suddenly a sound escaped from Champagne. It sounded like it was coming from the essence of her being.

Sharon continued to suck and lick until Champagne's body stopped quivering.

Zyair stood up. He wanted to kiss Champagne. He needed to be a part of this.

"Let me watch you fuck her," Sharon told him.

Champagne looked at Zyair. She sat up, took her dress off, and turned over. "Fuck me from behind." She looked at Sharon and told her, "You lay on the bed. I want to see what you taste like," surprising both Zyair and Sharon.

"You don't have to," Sharon told her.

"I want to."

Sharon looked at Zyair.

"If that's what she wants."

Sharon got undressed, and Zyair couldn't help but notice how similar her body was to Champagne's.

Champagne watched Zyair watch Sharon. She wasn't jealous because she knew that Sharon wasn't into men.

When Sharon lay on the bed, Champagne looked at her. "Let me know if I'm not doing this right."

"I'm sure you'll do just fine. Just do to me what you like done to you."

Champagne looked at Zyair and told him, "Give me a minute."

He stepped back and took his shirt and pants off. He watched while Champagne massaged Sharon's breasts and played with her nipples.

Champagne then started kissing Sharon. Her heart was racing, she was anxious. She wondered if she would like the taste of pussy or if it would turn her off. She had to find out. Sliding down Sharon's legs, she pulled Sharon to the edge of the bed and got on her knees.

Zyair took this as a sign and knelt as well.

Champagne placed her head between Sharon's legs and ran her tongue on the inside of Sharon's walls. Then she covered Sharon's pussy with her mouth.

"Do to me what you like," Sharon said.

Champagne started imitating how Zyair ate her pussy. She found, to her surprise, that she liked the taste. "Come on," she told Zyair, "put your dick in me."

He didn't' have to be told twice. He entered her with such force. He wanted her to know that he was the master of that pussy.

Champagne started pushing back.

He took that as a sign to fuck her harder. The harder

he fucked her, the more passionate she was in eating Sharon's pussy.

Sharon grabbed Champagne's head. "Shit, girl, are you sure you haven't done this before? You going to make me come all over that face."

On that note, Zyair looked up. He watched Sharon's face as she came all over Champagne's mouth, which made him come as well. He pushed his dick up as far as it would go in Champagne's pussy.

When he was done, he was surprised to find that he was still semi-hard.

Champagne felt like she was in another zone. She told Zyair, "Put it in my ass."

Still inside her, he asked, "Are you sure?"

"Come on, do it now before I change my mind."

He pulled out of her pussy, spread her cheeks apart, and slowly entered her ass, using her pussy juices as a lubricant. He was ecstatic, because she'd always told him, "The ass is a special treat."

They both closed their eyes.

Sharon climbed off the bed and sat on the floor. She was intrigued with what was going on as she watched Zyair move in and out of Champagne's ass real slow and steady. She placed her hands under Champagne and found her clitoris, and started pressing on it.

This made Champagne move along with Zyair, causing his dick to go in deeper.

"Awwww," Zyair kept repeating over and over, his eyes closed. "This feels so good."

Champagne couldn't speak. She was too busy enjoying the feel of Sharon's fingers and the pressure of Zyair's dick going in and out of her ass. They'd done this a couple of times before, but it was a while ago, and she'd forgotten how good it felt.

"I'm going to come again," Zyair yelled.

"I am too. Press harder, Sharon," Champagne said.

Sharon did as she was instructed.

Shortly after, Zyair and Champagne came together.

When it was done, he pulled out of Champagne real slow. "I'm going to the bathroom to get a rag. I'll be back."

When he left the room, Champagne lay and looked at Sharon, who was standing up. "You don't want to lay down?"

"No, I think I'm going to be leaving."

"You don't have to leave."

Sharon sat on the bed and rubbed Champagne's face. "Thank you."

"No, we should be thanking you."

Sharon bent over to kiss Champagne.

They were so deep into the kiss that neither of them noticed when Zyair walked in the room. He stood there with the rag in his hand and watched them. When they pulled away from one another, he walked over and handed Champagne a warm rag.

He looked at Sharon. "Do you want to take a shower?"

"That would be nice."

After wiping and sitting up, Champagne said, "I'll show her where everything is."

That night after Sharon left, as Zyair and Champagne lay in bed, he asked her, "Did you enjoy it?"

"Yes, but I was concerned about you."

This surprised Zyair. He didn't think Champagne realized he was in the room half the time. "I'm glad to hear that because emotionally I was messed up. One on hand I wanted it to stop, then I didn't want it to stop. I wasn't sure how involved or uninvolved I should be."

"Well, whatever decision you made was the right one."

He moved closer to her and wrapped his arms around her, and together they spooned. "I have to tell you what made me feel better was when you allowed us to have anal sex in front of her. That made me feel like I was a priority."

As an afterthought, he added, "You know how rare it is when you give me the ass."

Champagne laughed. *I wonder if things will ever be the same between us.*

Zyair was thinking, *This shit will not happen again.*

CHAPTER TWENTY-FOUR
"USED TO BE MY GIRL"
O'JAYS

It had finally happened, and neither knew what to say to the other. A couple of days had gone by, and Champagne wondered if she should pretend like it meant nothing. She didn't know if that was something she could do. The lovemaking was good as hell between her and Sharon, and between her and Zyair afterwards. She knew immediately that she was going to be looking for a female lover.

Does that make me gay? Champagne already asked herself that question a million times. In Jamaica, when they came back from Jamaica, while they were on the hunt, and now. Her answer was a definite no, but after watching an episode of *Oprah* that featured women who had been married for years and suddenly discovered they were gay, she wasn't too sure.

It's just a phase, that's all. Just a phase. She hoped she was right, and that's all it was.

She was in her office with the door closed when she heard Candy come in the front door. Truth be told, she was attracted to Candy, but it was an attraction that she had to keep under wraps.

"Candy, come into my office."

Candy walked in. "Yes?"

"Remember that business trip I told you about that I have to go on?'

"Yes."

"Well, I want you to go with me. After all, you did the majority of the research, and I believe it'll be good for you to actually meet the client and learn more about the foundation."

Candy liked that idea. She was ready to get away as well. She knew it was business, but being in Washington D.C. meant she just might get a chance to party.

"Is there anything you need me to do?" Candy asked.

"No. Just continue pricing the halls and hotels for Ms. Trina Houston."

Not only was Candy assisting Champagne in setting up a non-profit for one of her clients, but she was also helping in the planning of Trina Houston's wedding.

Trina was one of Champagne's money-making clients. She was getting married and starting a non-profit organization. Balancing the two was becoming a challenge, and she needed Champagne's expertise.

Champagne watched Candy leave the office and shut the door. She couldn't stop herself from wondering how good Candy ate pussy. *Stop it, girl. You know better than that.* She was feeling out of control with this whole sexuality thing. A door had been opened and she just couldn't seem to shut it.

Shay buzzed Champagne's phone. "There's a Sharon on the line."

Smiling, Champagne picked up. "Hey there."

"What's up, sexy?"

"Nothing. What's up with you?"

"Just thinking about you."

Shit, shit, shit! Champagne wondered what she was supposed to say to that. "Oh and what were you thinking?"

"How good you taste."

Before Champagne could stop herself, she asked, "When do you want to taste me again?"

"Mmmmmm . . . is that an invitation?"

This is my chance to take it back. "I don't know. Maybe."

"With or without Zyair?"

Champagne knew the answer was *without*, but would that mean she was cheating? Was it cheating when you slept with someone of the same sex?

"All you have to do is say the word," Sharon told her.

What the hell am I getting myself into?

Before Champagne could answer, Shay poked her head in the door. "Your appointment is here."

"Listen, is it all right if I call you back? Someone's here to see me."

Sharon told her that was fine.

Champagne felt a little relieved to be hanging up the phone. She was also glad her client was there to take her mind off whether she was a lesbian or turning into one. This obsession was becoming ridiculous even to her.

That night after Sharon left, Zyair had barely said a word. If anything, he was more distant. Champagne felt like he was pulling away. Was he, or was it her imagination?

The following day Zyair was in his office thinking about what had transpired. He wasn't sure how he felt it about it. On one hand, he was turned on, but on the other, he was glad it was over and definitely didn't want it to happen again. This incident with Sharon— that's what he was going to call it, an incident—just didn't sit right with him. Sharon seemed like she was into Champagne more than he would have liked. He had to admit, he felt threatened.

What happened in Hedonism was different because they were not on their home turf and it was spontaneous. The more Zyair thought about it, the more it seemed like Champagne had pressed the issue a bit too much. Did that say something about him as a man? Did that say something about his lovemaking?

After about half-hour he was ready for Sharon to get her ass out the house.

I mean, damn, how much kissing, tittie rubbing, and pussy-licking can one do?

He hoped this let-me-see-if-I'll-enjoy-making-love-to-a-woman-sober shit Champagne pulled on him was done with. That question should have been answered.

Zyair glanced at the clock. He was meeting with Da-Neen shortly to go over her business plan.

Knock, knock.

Zyair looked up to see DaNeen poking her head in the door.

"Is it all right if I come in?"

Zyair waved her in. "Come on." He couldn't help but notice how sexy she looked. He was noticing it more than usual. It wasn't just in what she wore, but there was something else about her. Maybe it was the confidence she carried because she was trying to do her thing.

Champagne's doing her thing too, he thought to himself, trying not to notice how high the slit was in her skirt. When she sat down, he thought he could almost see her panties.

DaNeen caught him looking and positioned herself so that he could see even more.

She'd been wanting this man for quite some time now. Everything about him turned her on. His gentleness and the way he handled people, his generosity, the way he treated his lady when she was around.

DaNeen wanted all those things to herself, and she was tired of waiting. She'd been watching him for over a year, trying to get close to him, but it just wasn't happening. Well, she was determined to make it happen, and not only one time. If it meant taking a chance and losing her self-respect, she was willing to do that. Because it's better to try and lose than to not try and not know if you would have won.

Bringing his attention to her face, Zyair said, "Let me see what you've done so far."

"Can I come around there and show you?" Her plan was to stand as close as possible to him and rub up against him if she could.

"Sure."

DaNeen walked around the desk and bent over while opening her folder, her breast resting on his arms.

Zyair felt himself responding. This was unusual for him. Normally he could keep his desire under control. He was going to blame it on Champagne. She was the one who opened Pandora's box.

He looked up at DaNeen. "You might want to back up some."

Placing her hand on the center of her breast, DaNeen said, "Oops, my bad."

For the next hour they went over her business plan, with Zyair suggesting some changes she might want to make. Throughout that hour, he noticed DaNeen's subtle touches. He knew she was doing it on purpose and was flattered by it. But being flattered and fucking around was a world apart. There was no way he was going to cheat on Champagne. He was just going to ignore her advances.

When DaNeen left the office, Zyair breathed a sigh of relief. He didn't know what was going on with him. He did know that it was dangerous. He needed someone to talk to. As usual, he called his boy Thomas.

"Yo, man, we need to talk," he said when Thomas answered the phone. "Stop by the office."

Thomas told him, "Okay."

The day progressed as usual, Zyair checking on the restaurant, mingling with the clientele, and watching DaNeen out of the corner of his eye. A couple of times when he looked up, he caught her looking his way.

A couple of hours later, Zyair was walking towards his office when he heard Thomas's voice. "Yo, man, wait up."

Zyair waited until he was beside him. They gave each other dap.

"So what's up? What do you want to talk about?"

"Wait until we get in my office, man."

When they stepped into the office, Zyair spilled the beans. "Man, it's DaNeen."

Thomas's eyes got real wide. "Don't tell me you fucked her."

"Nah, man, you know me better than that."

"Are you about to fuck her?"

"No."

"You want to fuck her?"

The look on Zyair's face gave Thomas his answer.

"I knew it, I knew it, I knew it."

Zyair knew it too. Thomas had warned him about her. He remembered him saying, "She wants you, man. Don't get yourself stuck in the wrong situation. That's what gets people in trouble, situations."

Sitting on the oversized chair, Thomas asked, "So what are you going to do about it?"

"I don't know."

"What do you mean, you don't know? Does that mean you're considering stepping out on your lady?"

"Nah."

"Then what you call me for? To share with me the fact that you think somebody is cute?"

Zyair started laughing. "I know, it's just that"—Zyair threw his hands up—"You know what, never mind. I'm tripping, that's all."

"You see, that's what your ass get for hiring some-body as fine as her. You want me to ask her out?"

Zyair, a dead-ass serious look on his face, sat next to Thomas. He leaned over and placed his elbows on his knees. "If I tell you something real personal, you better not tell any of the boys."

Thomas smacked his leg and jumped up. "I knew it. You did fuck her."

Growing frustrated, Zyair told him, "No."

"Then what the hell is it? You're getting on my damn nerves, acting all secretive and shit. Out with it."

"I let another woman eat Champagne's pussy."

Thomas sat down. "Repeat that."

"I let another woman—"

Thomas didn't let him finish. "You're lying."

"No, I'm not."

Thomas just wasn't believing him. "When?"

"A couple of days ago."

"Oh shit!"

Zyair was expecting more of a reaction. "Oh shit? That's it?"

"What more do you want me to say? I'm in shock. I didn't think Champagne would be down with something like that."

"This ain't the first time."

"What? And you're just now telling me?"

Zyair went on to tell him about Hedonism.

"I told you, you would turn into freaks going there."

Zyair wanted to tell him how he was feeling all crazy now, like maybe they'd done the wrong thing.

"Give me details."

"Hell no. So you can sit around and fantasize about my woman? You must be out of your mind."

Thomas all of a sudden got dreamy-eyed. "I wonder if Alexis is into women?"

Zyair playfully knocked Thomas upside the head.

That night, while Zyair and Champagne lay in the bed reading, Zyair decided he wanted to bring it up. He sat his book down.

"Champagne?"

She looked up from her book. "Yes?" From the look on Zyair's face, she could tell he was in serious mode. She didn't feel like talking. She just wanted to read her book.

"Will you put your book down? I need to talk to you about something."

Champagne turned the book over on her lap. "Go ahead."

"It's just that we haven't talked about what transpired the other night."

Shit, I knew this was going to happen. "What is there to talk about? It's done and over with."

"Is it?"

How can he possibly know? "Yes, Zyair, it is."

For some inexplicable reason, he didn't believe her. What was he to do about it? Nothing. All he could do was take her word and hope to hell she meant what she was saying.

"Did you enjoy it?"

"Yes, Zyair, I did."

Zyair didn't like the tone of her voice. She was acting like he was bothering her. "Damn, Champagne, all I want to do is talk about it."

"We didn't do all this talking after it happened In Jamaica."

"That's another country. This is in-house."

"What difference does it make?"

"It makes a hell of a difference."

"Why?"

Zyair took Champagne's hand. "Listen, I'm going to keep it real with you. I'm feeling a little insecure. I didn't think it would affect me this way, but it has. And I need some reassurance that it was an 'us' thing and a one-time thing."

Champagne wanted to tell him it was. She wanted to mean it when she said it.

"I love you, Zyair, and nothing can change that."

They both wondered if she was being honest or trying to convince them both.

CHAPTER TWENTY-FIVE
"KEEP ON MOVIN' "
SOUL II SOUL

"You know I have to go away for four days, right?" Alexis said to Champagne as they sat in Alexis's living room. "I'll be away when you return. Khalil and I are going to Cancun."

Every time Alexis said his name, it irritated the hell out of her, especially with what she now knew. She wanted so bad to tell her, but she needed to get some hard evidence first.

"Really? Whose idea was that?"

"His."

If Alexis could smile any harder, Champagne thought she would throw up. On one hand she was glad for her friend, but damn, why couldn't this joy come from some-one else? Ashamed of the way she was feeling and ready to take action, Champagne told Alexis she had to leave.

Alexis wasn't fooled. "When I come back, we need to talk."

Champagne looked at her. "About what?"

"Us."

Champagne told her, "We'll do that."

The second Champagne got into her car, she picked up the phone to call Zyair.

She thought to herself, *Alexis has really lost her mind behind this Khalil fellow.* Then again, who was she to talk about someone losing their mind? She was thinking about sleeping with women.

When Champagne spoke to Zyair, all he had to say was, "You really need stay out of this."

Do I really want to get involved? Should I mind my own business? Not only that, but I know Zyair is going to be pissed that I got his friend involved.

She tried to convince herself that she was doing the right thing because her friend was in trouble, and it was her duty to step up to the plate and do what she had to do to help out.

After Thomas told her about Khalil being a porn star and going to swingers clubs, her concerns grew because she knew they were having sex. Alexis let that one slip out.

Freak it, I'm going to call Thomas, and we're going to get to the bottom of this.

When Champagne arrived at her office, she picked up the phone and dialed Thomas's number. It went straight to his answering service.

"Thomas, it's Champagne. Call me at my office. I wanted to speak with you about Alexis and the bad man." She laughed to herself when she said "the bad man." Champagne wondered why this was becoming a mission to her. The "save Alexis" mission.

Champagne stood up and walked over to the window and watched the people below. She wondered where they going, what they did every day, if anyone of them were struggling in there personal lives, their sexual lives. She knew she wasn't the only person in the world having these same sex thoughts. If you watched television, listened to the radio, or went to the bookstore, it seemed like sexuality had become a hot topic. It seemed like a small portion of the world was what most called "straight." That term cracked her up because it implied the other group of people were "crooked."

Champagne thought about when she and Alexis were younger and how they "played" with one another. Is that something all young girls did? Damn, she wished she had someone she could ask. She wondered, was it out of curiosity that they explored one another's body, or was her sexuality being formed? She wondered did they both turn out heterosexual because it's what they were supposed to do? She did remember that it felt good and that there were days when she couldn't wait for Alexis to come over so they could "do it."

It started when they were in the fourth grade and continued until they got to middle school. That's when life changed and boys became a big part of their life.

Damn, this is some deep shit. I might have been gay back then and due to life circumstances and wanting to be like everyone else, I went the other way.

Champagne realized she'd blocked this memory, or pushed it so far back in her mind. She wondered if Alexis had done the same. She couldn't even remember when they stopped or how they stopped. Was it discussed, or was it just over?

Maybe this is why I'm bugging out over this relationship with Khalil. Zyair said I was acting jealous. I think I am.

With this revelation, Champagne had to go back to her desk and sit down. She needed to think, was she in love with Alexis. *Nah, that's not it. I'm thinking too hard about this whole thing.*

On that note, her cell phone rang. She pulled it out

of her purse, flipped it open, and looked at the ID. It was Thomas. She pressed the accept button. "Hello?"

"Hey, you," Thomas said. "I got your message. What's up?"

"I thought I left a message for you to call me at my office?"

"Does it really matter what phone I called you on?"

"You don't have to get smart."

"You know what, you're right. I apologize. I just have a lot on my mind today."

Champagne could understand that. "I know what you mean."

"So what's up?"

"I want to do what we talked about?"

"What?"

Exasperated, Champagne said, "You know . . . follow Khalil."

"Really?"

"Yeah. Find out from your friend when he goes or if she can get any information, and we can get the ball rolling."

"I will, but let me ask you this, do you have a plan? How are we going to do this? Are we going to go in the place, and if we see him what happens then? I'm sure we can't take cameras in there."

Champagne hadn't thought that deep into it. One thing she did know is that she wasn't too keen about going inside.

"Maybe we can sit outside and take pictures of him coming and going."

"That'll be an all-night thing. What if he's not even there?"

"Well, shit, Thomas, I don't know. Why don't you come up with something? You're the one who's always talking about Alexis is going to be your wife. Come up with something to save your wife."

Thomas was quiet.

"Thomas, are you there?"

"Yeah, yeah, I'm thinking. Listen, give me an hour and I'll call you back."

"Okay."

After they hung up, Champagne asked herself, *Why? Why am I doing this?*

An hour later Thomas called back. "Okay, here's what we're going to do. I called my girl, and she said they have friends in common, so she's going to make a couple of phone calls and get some information."

"Does she know why we're doing this? Would she be doing it if she knew you wanted Alexis?"

"Don't worry about all that. I got this."

Champagne hung up and wondered how they were going to pull it off. *Okay, I'm not going to think about it. I'm going to just focus on work.*

Pressing the intercom button, she called Candy into the office.

"Yes?"

"Are you packed and ready?"

Candy started laughing. "The truth? I always wait until the last minute to pack. If I try to pack earlier, I have too many options and end up getting frustrated."

"You know we only have a couple more days until we leave."

"Yeah, I know."

Champagne told her, "Listen, I'm stepping out for a moment. Hold down the fort."

"As always," Candy said, wondering where she was going.

Before Champagne could say another word, her cell

phone started ringing. She glanced at the ID. It was Thomas.

She pressed the accept button. "Damn, didn't we just get off the phone?"

"Check it, we can do this tonight."

Moving the phone from her mouth, Champagne told Candy, "That's all." She waited until Candy left the office to say, "You mean, go to the swingers club?"

"Yeah, I was told he'll be there tonight."

"You're lying." Champagne couldn't believe it was happening this fast. There was no way in the world the same day they came up with the plan that they could see it through. Shit just wasn't this easy.

"Listen, do you want to do this or not? You need to let me know so I can plan accordingly."

"How? What exactly is the plan?"

"Let's figure that out when we get together later."

They made arrangements to meet at eleven that night at her office. Champagne had to come up with something to tell Zyair. For her to up and leave in the middle of the night would definitely cause some suspicion. Hopefully, this would be one of those nights he stayed at the restaurant real late. If not, she'd tell him one of her clients was having a party in the city and she had to attend.

"Well, this is certainly last-minute," Zyair responded when she told him the lie.

"I know. Initially I wasn't going to attend, but she practically begged me." Champagne told him that one of her former clients was considering switching to her company and wanted to speak with her after a dinner party she was having. There was no way in the world she could tell him what she and Thomas was up to, and she'd told Thomas not to say anything either.

He wasn't too keen on lying to his boy, but Champagne convinced him that if he didn't even mention it, he wouldn't be lying.

It worked out anyway, because Zyair was staying at the restaurant late.

That night while getting ready, Champagne changed clothes numerous times, all the while wondering, how Thomas knew beyond a shadow of a doubt that Khalil was going to be there.

All he would tell her is, "I've got connections."

Well, so be it. As long they got the evidence they needed she could care less.

The plan was as follows. Thomas and Champagne would meet up at her office. From there, she would get in his car, and they would go to the spot.

Champagne's stomach was in her chest. Her instincts told her, "Don't do this," but she couldn't stop herself. It's like a force was pulling her to do the unthinkable.

When they arrived at the club, they would walk in together as a couple. There was a rule there that no man could go in alone. He had to be accompanied by a woman.

Walking in unfamiliar surroundings with nakedness everywhere, this was the part that scared her. She knew she wouldn't feel comfortable walking in a place with her man's best friend and people all around making love or doing whatever it is they do. She expressed this to Thomas, who told her not to worry about it, they could go their separate ways.

Of course he had his reasons. He wanted to see what he could come back and get into without it being awkward. Two, she was his best friend's girl, and as it stood, they were going behind his back.

"We'll do a walk-through and see if we spot him," Thomas told her.

"What will we do if we see him? We can't just walk up on him and yell out, 'Busted.' "

"No, we can't, but what I can do is make sure he sees me. Then when you have another dinner party, and he sees me again, I'll handle the rest."

If they weren't on the telephone, Champagne knew she'd throw her arms around him and kiss him on the cheek. He was doing this not only because he thought he was in love with Alexis, but because of her as well. She knew this and would let him know she knew.

The evening flew by, and Champagne finally decided on what to wear. She didn't want to dress sexy or appear too dressed up or down. After all, she was supposed to be at a dinner party.

As agreed upon, they met at Champagne's office. He called her from around the corner, and she met him outside.

Climbing into his car, she asked him, "Are we sure we want to do this?"

"There's no turning back now," he told her. He glanced at what she wore and thought to himself that Zyair was a lucky man. "You look nice."

Champagne smiled and thanked him. She closed the door, relaxed in her seat, and placed her head on the headrest.

Thomas pulled off slowly and asked her, "Why are we doing this again?"

"I keep asking myself the same thing. All I'm coming up with is, there's something about him that doesn't sit right. It's just an instinct, and I only want what's best for my girl and I don't think it's him."

"Isn't this the kind of thing that breaks up friendships, when people butt in?"

Champagne looked at him and crossed her arms. "Well, you're butting in. Why are you butting in?"

"Because I love her."

If it was any other time, Champagne would have laughed, but there was a seriousness to his tone.

When she didn't make a crack, Thomas asked her, "You don't have anything to say?"

Champagne shook her head. "You know, we all do things, feel things, and say things we can't explain sometimes. They are just what are. Who am I to judge?"

Thomas knew she was speaking about other things, but he didn't feel it was his place to pry. But he did have something else he needed to know. "Let me ask you something."

"Go ahead."

"What is it about me you don't like? I want you to be honest with me too, because I know whatever you say is probably what Alexis is thinking."

"It's not that I don't like you. I don't want you to think that. I care for you a lot, Thomas. You're like a brother to Zyair. Therefore, you're like a brother to me."

"Then why do I feel that way? Sometimes when I come over I feel unwanted. I don't know what I'm stepping into when I see you, if you're going to be in one of your happy, welcome-to-my-house or one of your get-out moods."

Champagne didn't realize she behaved that way. Okay, yes, sometimes he pissed her off with some of his sexist remarks and comments he made about women, but she didn't not like him, and she wanted him to know that, especially with what he was doing for her today.

She positioned herself so that she could face him. "Thomas, please hear this. I do like you. It's just that

sometimes when the fellows are around, I get insecure."

"But why take it out on me?"

"I don't mean to take it out on you. You're one of the
connections to Zyair's player past, and sometimes
when I hear you two talking you make it sound like
he's missing out on something. That's the last thing I
want him to think."

Thomas was real quiet as he contemplated on his response. Did he tell her how much he admired what she
and Zyair shared, that he wanted the same thing for
himself? Did he tell her that sometimes he didn't feel
worthy and that he wondered if he would be able to be
the type of man a woman wanted and needed? He
chose not to say those things. Instead he said, "Listen,
Zyair loves you, and nothing I say out of ignorance or
out of anything else will change that. If anything, he's
the one that's telling me what I'm missing, that I need
to settle down and find the one. I envy what you guys
have. I would never jeopardize that. Although, my
bringing you here to the house of swingers just might
do that."

It was then that Champagne realized they were in
the parking garage.

"You do know he'd kick my ass, right?" Thomas
turned off the car.

Champagne didn't want to answer that.

Thomas wasn't done yet. "Let me ask you this, does
Alexis have any idea how much I want her?"

Champagne didn't have the heart to tell him that although Alexis had made comments about how good-
looking he is, she thought he was a straight-up dog.
"She does, but if you want her to take you serious, you
need to be more serious and stop acting a male whore."

Thomas knew what she was saying was true. He was getting tired of playing the game and was also ready to step it up and step up to Alexis.

Climbing out the car, he told Champagne, "Come on, let's go catch this chump."

Champagne walked behind him. She could feel her body shaking in anticipation of what she might witness. "We are going our separate ways, right?"

"Yes, Champagne. We've gone over this a few times already."

"I know, but I'm trying to be sure of what we planned."

"If you see him, you're going make sure he sees you and then I'm going to have a dinner party and you're going to say something to him that'll make him stop seeing Alexis. But if I see him first, do you think I should approach him?"

Thomas removed her hand and placed his hands on her shoulders. "Get it together. Breathe or something."

Champagne started laughing because she realized she was having a meltdown.

This worried Thomas. "Maybe you need to sit in the car and let me handle this by myself."

Champagne didn't want that to happen. She had to admit, she was curious about what was going on inside. She'd heard so many tales about swingers, and now she wanted to see for herself. Maybe if she thought of it like Hedonism, it wouldn't be so bad. After all, they'd sat next to people having sex, and once you got over the initial shock, it become almost natural.

She grabbed his hand. "Come on, let's do this."

When they stepped up the door, there stood two of the biggest men Champagne had ever seen. They had to both be over 6 feet 5 inches and 300 pounds.

Goddamn, she thought.

The men frisked Thomas and looked Champagne over. She felt like they were looking inside her. The men allowed them to pass, and once inside, they showed their IDs and paid one hundred dollars to enter.

One hundred dollars, Champagne thought. *Not a lot to pay for a night of sex with anyone and in any way.*

Once they walked inside, there was a long hallway with numerous rooms on either side.

Thomas looked at her and asked, "Are you ready to go our separate ways?"'

"Not yet." She took his hand, and together they went towards the first room.

The first room must have been the "get acquainted" room. There was a lot of touching, laughing, and kissing. Basically people were sizing one another up. One of the things that surprised Champagne was that most of the people there looked like they could be your neighbor or co-worker. A couple of them looked like they could be your parents.

Champagne laughed to herself. It was obvious kinkiness didn't discriminate.

"Are you ready to separate?" Thomas asked.

"Yep, I'm thinking I can handle it."

Little did she know, in the next room two women were laying side by side, caressing one another. They were lost in their own world, with their tongues meeting, eyes closed. Champagne found them to be attractive. Both had athlete bodies. One was Puerto Rican and the other Black. Champagne always associated these places with white folks. Boy, was she wrong.

Glancing around the room, she counted three others, two men and another female. The others were drinking and observing. She watched as one of the men walked over and knelt down beside the women. They opened their eyes and pulled him in. The Black woman caught Champagne's eyes and beckoned her over.

There was no way in the world Champagne was going over there. Instead she averted her eyes, and when she felt the woman look away, she looked at them again.

The man was placing himself between the Puerto Rican's legs. He cupped her ass and pulled up her to meet his dick, which was already covered with a condom.

At least they come prepared. Champagne couldn't pull away, and when he plunged into the woman, she instantly became moist.

A man whispered in Champagne's ear, "Why don't you take off your dress?" and ran his hand across her ass.

Champagne took that as a sign to leave the room. She was about to turn the corner when someone grabbed her and threw her up against the wall.

"So this is what you do?"

Champagne was staring in Jackson's face. She couldn't help but look down and notice the outline of a hard dick on his briefs. She looked up at him and the smirk on his face. *This shit is going from bad to worse.* "Take your hands off me."

Jackson pressed up against her and pushed her body into the wall. "You could come here, but you can't give me any pussy." He looked around. "Where's your man?"

Champagne was getting ready to panic. Then she saw someone's fingers reach around Jackson's neck and pull him off her.

It was Thomas, and he looked ready to tear Jackson's ass apart. "Get your hands off her now."

Jackson landed against the wall across from where they stood.

Thomas looked at Champagne. "You all right?"

Champagne nodded.

"I always knew you were a whore." Jackson looked like he was ready to charge Thomas.

Thomas turned to face him. "Don't even think about it."

Why is this happening? This is what I get for even being here. Champagne grabbed Thomas by the arm. "Let's get out of here."

By this time, security had arrived and told everyone they needed to leave the premises.

Jackson had to get his final words in. "Don't think this will be the last time you see me."

Thomas stood in his face. "Are you fucking threatening her?"

Jackson wasn't backing down. "You don't look like that Zyair fellow to me."

Champagne pulled Thomas. "Come on, ignore him. Let's go."

Security escorted them to the door.

Once they were outside, Thomas asked Champagne, "Who was that asshole?"

"That was my old boss."

Thomas tilted his head and frowned. "Your boss?"

"Yeah. Now you see why I quit? He was always throwing himself on me, and it just got to be too much.

"Does Zyair know about this?"

"No. I was able to handle it."

In exasperation, Thomas asked, "Why do women do that?"

"Do what?"

"Not tell their men when someone is harassing them? Why do you ladies think it's your job to handle it?"

"I don't speak for all women. I speak only for myself. It's not that I think it's my job to handle anything. If I can, I will, and if I can't, then I'll hand it over."

As they were walking towards the garage, they heard a car slam on brakes. Looking up, neither could make out the person inside the car. It was DaNeen.

What the hell? DaNeen was on her way home from hanging out with her girls in the city. She was driving by the garage when she spotted Thomas and Champagne. Of course, she knew who they were. She knew who anyone was that played an important part in Zyair's life.

She glanced around to see if Zyair was on the premises. Then she remembered, he was staying at the restaurant late that night, and if she recalled correctly, she thought she'd overheard him saying to someone that Champagne had a dinner date with a client. His best friend certainly didn't look like a client to her.

She was definitely going to use this bit of information to her own advantage. Earlier that week, she'd asked Zyair if he would go with her to a meeting with a potential client. She didn't ask him because she didn't know what she was doing. She'd asked him because she wanted some time with him. She wanted him to be impressed with her smarts and her capabilities. Then she would take him out to dinner and seduce his ass. She knew Champagne would be out of town because he'd mentioned that as well.

DaNeen couldn't help wondering what his woman and his best friend were doing out in the middle of the night, and why would Champagne lie about her whereabouts?

*   *   *

On the drive to her office, Thomas told her he didn't
see Khalil. He didn't tell her that he would probably be
going back there.

Champagne was disappointed that they didn't get
anything on him, and pissed that she'd worked herself
up into a frenzy over the whole thing.

"Maybe something else will come up," Thomas offered as a way to console her.

"Maybe this is God's way of telling us to let things
fall however they may. If Khalil is really who we think
he is, it'll eventually come out."

"You think so?"

"I don't know. It just sounded good saying it."

Thomas laughed.

When Champagne went to climb out of his car, he
placed his hand on top of hers. "Thanks, Champagne."

"For what?"

"For clearing up my misunderstanding."

"What misunderstanding?"

"You know, the fact that I thought you didn't like
me."

Champagne kissed him on the cheek. "You're welcome. I know you're a decent man, Thomas. You just
need to let others know it."

When Champagne arrived home, Zyair was laying
in the bed. "How did it go? Do you have a new client?'"

"I believe I do." Champagne started to undress. She
wanted to tell Zyair about the night's events. It was on
the tip of her tongue, but she decided to wait. She and
Thomas would tell him together.

She went into the bathroom to shower and brush
her teeth. She was horny and wanted to do something
about it.

Zyair called from the bed, "Are you about to take a shower?"

"Yes, and when I get out, it's on."

For a second there, he was curious about this impromptu shower, but after hearing that it was for a session of lovemaking, that curiosity faded.

While in the shower Champagne thought about the swingers club and what she'd witnessed. It surprised her that not everyone was naked, and that there were just as many people there observing as there were participating.

She thought about the two women and the man that were making love, and found her fingers making way to her pussy. She fondled with her hairs and looked up at the shower head. *I wonder if I can make myself come with that.* Yes, she and Zyair were going to make love, but there was nothing wrong with an extra orgasm.

She took the shower head down with her right hand and spread her legs just a little wider. She took her left hand and separated the skin just above her clitoris. Champagne closed her eyes and leaned back against the shower wall. She positioned the shower head so that the water would hit the top of her clitoris and immediately she felt her legs buckle. Champagne felt a moan coming on and tried to keep it low. She didn't want Zyair to hear her. She bought the shower head closer to her clitoris so the water could hit it harder. Her pussy walls pulsated, and it wasn't long before the buildup erupted and her orgasm hit hard, buckling her knees. She pressed her lips together and looked up at the ceiling. "Oh shit," she whispered.

After her orgasm, she completed her shower and stepped out. She dried off and went into the bedroom, where Zyair was laying back with his hands behind his head and his eyes closed.

Champagne, on her hands and knees, straddled him and kissed him on the lips. "Open your eyes," she told him.

He obliged.

She met his mouth with her tongue and licked his lips.

Zyair reached up for her, but she grabbed his hands and held them down to his side.

"I want to do all the work," she said.

Being the man he was, Zyair didn't object.

Champagne nibbled his neck and caressed his chest. Then she moved her hands down between his legs, cupping his balls.

"You're feisty tonight," he said. "What kind of dinner party was that?"

Champagne shushed him as her mouth made its way to his navel, where she dipped her tongue.

She knew she would be going away, she knew that she was wrong for lying to him and she knew she was wrong for her sexual thoughts that did not include him. She was going to make it up to him.

She then ran her tongue from his navel and stopped when she reached his dick. She looked at it and decided she wanted to devour it. She placed it in her mouth and covered the whole length of it. She felt it hit the back of her throat and slowly brought her mouth up and licked it with her tongue.

Zyair grabbed the back of her head and tried to push her back down.

She pushed his hands back into the bed. Looking up at him, she told him, "Let me do this my way." She licked all around his dick and pushed it straight up so that she could lick and suck on his balls. She went back and forth, from the left testicle to the right, and then tried to put both in her mouth while stroking his dick. She let her tongue fall under his balls and ran it from his balls to his ass and back up over and over again.

Zyair was squirming and moaning.

Champagne wanted him to do more. She went back up to his dick and placed it in his mouth, licking and sucking, sucking and licking. She licked the top half and stroked the bottom half, kissed around it and started sucking again.

"Oh, girl, you're going to make me come." Zyair grabbed her head again and tried to push his dick down her throat.

Champagne wasn't having it. She moved his hands and climbed on top of him. She straddled him and held herself up on her feet. She sat on his dick and started moving real slow up and down, squeezing her walls when she got up top and loosening them when she slammed their bodies together.

After doing this for a couple of minutes, she pressed down on him as hard as she could and started to grind. She knew that by doing this, not only she would come, but he would as well.

And that's what they both did. They ended the night with a kiss and a cuddle.

CHAPTER TWENTY-SIX
"ALL AROUND THE WORLD"
LISA STANSFIELD

It was now the day before the trip, and Candy was excited to be going to Chocolate City, especially since a couple of her friends lived there. Their plane was scheduled to leave Newark Airport at 5:30 p.m., and Candy was looking forward to the short first-class flight. She was also happy because her friend Elsie would be in town, and she would be able to set up some time to meet with her, perhaps for dinner.

Candy wasn't too sure what she should pack. She picked up the phone and called Champagne on her cell.

"Hello?"

"Hey, it's Candy."

"Are you packed yet?"

"That's why I was calling. I don't know what to pack."

"Well, you know we'll be gone for four days. Thursday, we have a meeting with Trina, Friday is the banquet, Saturday morning and early afternoon we'll be busy meeting with her wedding planner, and Sunday is a free day. So bring business casual, something dressy for the banquet, and whatever else you want to bring."

When they hung up, Candy went through her closet and picked out what she deemed proper. The one issue she encountered was the "something dressy" for the banquet. Instead of driving herself crazy over it, she decided to wait until she arrived in D.C. and hit the stores there. After all, she shopped well under pressure.

While on this adventure, she hoped to get to know Champagne better. In the office, everything was so tight and so businesslike. She wanted to get to know the woman she saw at Ladies First, the lady that was dancing, laughing, and having a good time.

Since her first day of employment, they had never addressed that night. It was like they never saw one another there. You would think it never happened. If Champagne wanted to keep it that way, that was fine, but Candy knew the real reason she and Zyair were there. It was the same reason most couples came to female gay clubs, to get their freak on or for foreplay. She also had a feeling that the person named Sharon who called the office often was more than an acquaintance. It was apparent in Champagne's behavior when they were on the phone together.

Champagne had finished her packing so she could have some time with Zyair before she left.

That night they were out to dinner. Zyair was sitting across from Champagne, taking her in with his eyes. Sometimes it amazed him that she still looked as good as the day they met. The intense attraction he had for her was still there, and he wondered if it would always be. He'd heard that it comes in spurts, the attraction and the love.

I love this girl so much. Why are we putting off the inevitable? It's time to set a date. "Champagne?"

"Yes?" Champagne looked up from her dessert menu.

"When are we going to set a date?"

"A date for what?"

"For us to get married."

This is not what I want to discuss the day before I leave. "Why are you asking me that now?"

"It's something I've been thinking about for a while now, and I'm ready."

Now you're ready, just when I've just started exploring sexually. "I thought we were going to wait a couple of years."

Zyair tilted his head and frowned. He felt as though Champagne was fighting him on this. Leaning across the table, he asked her, "What? You don't want to get married now?"

"I didn't say all that."

"Then what are you saying? Why put it off, if it's what we both want? I don't get it."

"There's nothing to get or not to get, Zyair. I just hadn't given it any thought. The last time we even discussed this, we both agreed that we would wait a couple more years, after your new restaurant was open, and I decided what I wanted to do businesswise."

Zyair had to admit, she was right. That was what they'd agreed upon. But a person was entitled to change his mind, and he told her this.

"Zyair, can we talk about this when I get back?"

"Why can't we talk about it now?"

"Because . . ."

"Because? Now you and I both know that is not a good answer. What? You don't want to marry me now?"

"Why are you jumping to conclusions?"

Zyair didn't understand what the hell was going on. He felt like he was begging her to marry him. A woman is the one that should to want to get married. She should be the one anxious to set a date. She should be the one asking him, are they going to continue on like this forever.

Interrupting his thoughts, Champagne said, "Zyair, it's not that I don't want to get married. You just need to understand that I've gotten comfortable in our relationship the way we are, and yes, I admit, maybe that's not a good thing. It's just that when you look at relationships now, marriage isn't really a big deal. People live together, create futures, and have kids without a ring."

Even though she didn't exactly say it, what Zyair heard was, "I don't want to marry you."

"You know what"—Zyair signaled for the waiter to come over—"let's just drop it. If you don't want to set a date, you don't have to. You just need to know that I'm ready to get married, and I'm ready to set a date."

Champagne wondered if this meant that he would be willing to leave her if she wasn't ready. It's not that she wasn't ready. If he'd said something about setting a date a couple of months ago, she just may have done that. She didn't even know why she was so resistant.

"Okay, when I get back, we'll start thinking about a date," she said, wanting to change the subject.

The waiter approached the table. "Are you ready for dessert?"

Champagne was, but she could tell that Zyair was ready to leave.

"No, thank you. Just bring us the check."

They rode home in silence.

Every time Champagne tried to make conversation, Zyair would speak in short sentences, which only left her frustrated. It was a relief when her cell phone rang.

Zyair glanced over at her when she picked it up.

Without looking at the caller ID, Champagne answered, "Hello."

"What's up, sexy?" Sharon said.

Champagne snuck a quick glance at Zyair who was pretending he wasn't listening.

"Nothing. Do you mind if I call you back?" Champagne was trying not to sound too personal.

"Are you busy?"

"Yes."

After a short pause, Sharon told her, "Sure, call me when you're alone."

The second Champagne hung up the phone, Zyair asked her, "Who was that?"

This threw her off because he never asked her who she was talking to. "It was a client," she lied, knowing he would be upset if she said it was Sharon.

"Did I hear a client say, 'Hey, sexy'?"

Oh shit, he heard that? "That's not what you heard. What they said was, 'Hey, Champagne.' "

Zyair wasn't crazy. He was almost certain that's what's he heard, but he didn't want to argue about it because there was a slight chance he could be wrong. After all, the phone wasn't up to his ear and he was trying to listen a bit too hard. This wasn't something he normally did, but things had changed once again between them and he was concerned.

"You don't have to believe me. I know who was on the phone, and I know what was said."

"Whatever you say, Champagne."

This wasn't the energy Champagne wanted to leave Zyair with. She knew she needed to reset the tone once they arrived home, but looking over at Zyair she knew that it wasn't going to be easy bringing him out from where he was mentally. Sex was almost always the answer, but she just wasn't up to it tonight.

When they pulled into the garage, they both climbed out the car without saying a word and went into the house. Zyair headed for his office, and Champagne for the bedroom. He just needed some space, and she was going to finish packing.

The following morning when she woke up, she was surprised to find that Zyair didn't sleep in bed with her. She knew for sure that he would come to his senses when he realized she was leaving the next day and would make up with her. If not that, at least come cuddle.

No such luck.

When she walked into the kitchen he was cooking breakfast for two.

Before she could get a word out, he walked over to her and pulled her into him. "I love you, and I apologize for acting like an ass last night."

This caught her off guard. All of a sudden she was overcome with emotion.

Zyair pulled away. "Why are you crying?"

"I don't know. I've just been feeling so overwhelmed lately, and then last night I couldn't find the right words to say to you."

Zyair cut her off. "Let's not talk about that now. Let's just enjoy breakfast and each other's company. When you get back, we'll deal with other things."

Champagne wondered how many things they would

have to deal with. She hoped this business trip would give her an opportunity to think about what direction she was headed in, with the thoughts she'd been having. On second thought, maybe she needed to spend a weekend in a spa. That way she'd be more relaxed and be able to clear her head.

CHAPTER TWENTY-SEVEN
"RUMORS"
TIMEX SOCIAL CLUB

When Candy arrived at the airport, it was a little after 4:00 p.m. Champagne was already there and noticed Candy as soon as she walked up.

"Hey, lady." Champagne patted the seat next to her.

Candy placed her small luggage on the floor and sat down. "Girl, this airport traveling and getting settled thing is a pain in the ass."

"I know that's right."

Candy wasn't one to chat when on the plane. She liked to be left alone to read, sleep, or listen to her music. She decided to see what kind of traveler Champagne was. "Okay, we need to get this out the way."

Champagne looked at her. "What?"

"Do you like to talk and have conversation when you're traveling, or do you want to be left alone?"

Champagne started laughing. "I know where you're going. Girl, I'm one of those leave-me-alone-and-let-me-be people as well. You don't have to worry about me talking you to death."

Candy placed her hand on her chest and said, "Whew! You don't know how relieved I am."

"Do you want to discuss our itinerary before we get on the plane?"

"Yeah, we can do that."

Champagne bent over and picked up her briefcase. She pulled out two pieces of paper and handed one to Candy.

For the next hour or so, they went over their plans for the weekend. This way Candy would know what was expected of her and when she was required to be around.

Candy was glad they did that, because she didn't want this to be the one and only business trip she was allowed to go on.

The plane ride was uneventful and short. When they landed, they headed to the hotel and agreed to have drinks together that night. After drinks Candy was going to meet up with Elsie, and Champagne was going to have dinner with her client.

In her hotel room, Champagne picked up the phone to call Alexis. There was no answer. She then called Zyair, and when he didn't answer, she decided to go downtown and shop. After all, she had a couple of hours to kill before she and Candy met up for a drink.

Zyair was sitting at a table in his restaurant with Thomas. They were discussing Champagne and Alexis.

DaNeen was across the room, watching and trying to read their lips because whatever they were talking about had them both looking intense. Ever since she'd seen Champagne and Thomas out that night, she wanted to tell Zyair, but the time just never seemed right. She wanted them to be alone, and for him to be so devastated that he fell into her arms. What would be ideal was for her to make this happen while Champagne was away.

She tried to read Zyair's lips as he told Thomas, "I asked her when we were going to set a date, and she all but said we weren't."

Although Zyair pretended that everything was kosher with Champagne prior to her leaving, it really wasn't. He was having serious doubts about where they stood. He thought things were getting better between them, that their going to Jamaica and experimenting was going to bring them closer together.

"Did she say those words to you?"

"No, she didn't have to. I could feel it."

"Man, that's some bullshit. Sometimes what we think a person means is not what they mean at all. I would not go on a feeling. When she comes back, you and her need to sit down and really talk, figure out what's going on."

"I feel like it's my entire fault for allowing someone else into our bedroom. Between that and Hedonism, we fucked up."

Thomas didn't have anything to say on that subject. He himself wished he could set up something like that with someone.

"Nah, you don't need a drink. It's just that." He hesitated. "You know I've got feelings for Alexis, right?"

"That's what you've been telling me for years."

"Well, I'm ready to make my move."

"What are you talking about, man? Why are you coming to me with this?"

"Because you're my boy, and I don't know who else to go to."

Zyair didn't respond.

Thomas went on, "I'm ready to settle down and change my ways. I'm ready to have what you and Champagne have."

"You mean *had*."

"No, *have*. No matter what you think is going on, you and Champagne belong together. I want to belong to someone like that, and I believe that person is Alexis."

"You're serious, aren't you?"

"As a heart attack."

"Well, why haven't you asked her out before now?"

"I wasn't ready."

"What makes you . . ." Zyair's voice trailed off along with his eyes.

Thomas followed his gaze and noticed Champagne's ex-boss, Jackson, and an attractive female walking towards them. *Fuck! Fuck! Fuck! I hope he doesn't say anything about seeing me and Champagne at the spot.*

Jackson put out his hand for Zyair to shake. "Zyair."

Zyair never really liked Jackson. He believed there was something underhanded and slimy about him. Not wanting to be an asshole, he shook his hand.

Then Jackson turned towards Thomas. "Funny seeing you here."

Zyair looked at Thomas. "You two know each other?"

Aw shit, here it comes. Thomas wasn't stupid. He knew to be prepared for anything.

"Your woman knows him too."

Zyair looked confused. "Of course she knows him. He's my boy."

Jackson knew immediately that Zyair wasn't up on the fact that "his boy" and Champagne were at a swingers club together the other night.

"Yo, man, why don't you step?" Thomas said.

Turning towards his date, Jackson told her, "Go have a seat. I'll be right with you in a minute."

By now Thomas had stood up. "I asked you to step."

Zyair stood up as well. "What the hell is going on?"

"Oh your boy didn't tell you he and your girl were out together the other night?"

Zyair looked at Thomas and could see guilt written all over his face. "What the hell is he talking about, Thomas?"

Thomas, caught between a rock and a hard place, felt like he had no choice but to tell Zyair what he and Champagne were up to.

Jackson was amused by what was going on, "Oh, so your boy didn't tell you they were at a swingers club?"

Zyair frowned. "Man, what the hell is he talking about?" He looked at Jackson. "Word is bond—You need to get up out of my restaurant and stop with the bull-shit."

"You think I'm bullshitting? Ask your boy. No, as a matter of fact, where was your girl Friday night?"

Thomas couldn't even punch Jackson in the mouth because he spoke the truth, and looking at Zyair, he could tell he was counting back the days.

Jackson laughed. "Let me leave you two alone."

Zyair signaled for security. Without taking his eyes off Thomas, he nodded towards Jackson and told them to escort him out.

Jackson followed them out with a smirk on his face. "Don't hate the player," he said. "You just got caught up in the game."

Zyair faced Thomas with fire in his eyes. "You need to tell me what he's talking about."

"It's not what you think, man."

Raising his voice, Zyair asked, "What do you mean,

it's not what I think? What the fuck are you talking about?" He started pacing the floor. "Please tell me you were not at a swingers club with my woman. Please tell me she didn't lie to me about where she was going."

The look on Thomas's face told him all he needed to know. If he was going to speak, he needed to speak fast. "It's not what you think, man. We went looking for Khalil. Diamond told me that he hung out there, and that's where she knew him from."

Before Thomas could even finish, Zyair's fist came out of nowhere and punched him in the mouth. All Thomas could do was stand there with his hand over his mouth.

Zyair's stance was one of "I'm about to kick your whole ass, muthafucka."

Security was right back on spot, with DaNeen following close behind.

Thomas threw his arms up. "I'm out, I'm out." He started to walk away, but then turned around to face Zyair. "Man, you really need to hear me out. I would never do anything to hurt you. You need to believe that."

"Just get out my face before I fuck you up."

Thomas knew the best thing to do was leave and deal with the situation later. He also knew he needed to call Champagne as soon as possible and let her know what was up.

CHAPTER TWENTY-EIGHT
"SECRET LOVERS"
ATLANTIC STARR

It was their last night in D.C. and Candy and Champagne were ordering drinks at the bar. Champagne's phone rang, and she looked at the caller ID. It was Thomas. *I wonder what he wants.*

"Excuse me," she told Candy. "I have to take this call." Champagne stood up and went towards the ladies' room. "Hello?"

"It's Thomas. What's up?"

"Nothing."

Not one to beat around the bush, Thomas came out with it. "Zyair knows about us going to the swingers club."

"What?" Champagne knew he didn't just say what she thought he did.

"Jackson came into the restaurant and caused a scene, and Zyair punched me in the mouth."

"Hold up, hold up. What do you mean, Jackson came into the restaurant? Did you tell him why we were there? Did you try to explain?" She was panicking, wondering what Zyair could be thinking right now. Should she call him, or should she wait until she arrived home to talk to him? *Shit! Shit! Shit!*

"What was I suppose to say Champagne? I tried to tell him what Diamond told me about Khalil, but he wasn't trying to hear a word of it and I can't say I blame him. Shit! I knew we shouldn't have went there together. This is fucked up. I may have lost my boy over this bullshit."

Champagne couldn't think of a word to say. She was trying to figure out what she was going to say to Zyair. What was there to say? All she could do was tell the truth. After all, she really didn't do anything wrong, but she knew he wouldn't understand. He'd already warned her to mind her business. *Fuck it, it's going to be what it's going to be.*

"Do you think I should call him or wait until I get home?"

"Yeah, I think you should, Champagne. You also need to know that he thinks you don't want to marry him."

Champagne didn't have to ask what gave him that impression. She already knew she was to blame. Damn it, what the hell was wrong with her? She'd been losing her mind lately. Was it really worth it? Was it worth losing Zyair?

"Thomas, thanks for giving me a heads-up. I'll call him and try to set things straight, although I don't think it's going to happen over the phone."

"Well, let me know if you need me."

As Champagne walked towards the table, Candy studied her facial expression.

Champagne sat down. She called the bartender over and ordered a shot of Patron.

"Damn, you ain't playing," Candy told her.

Champagne didn't respond.

"What's up? Is everything okay."

Needing to talk it out with someone, Champagne said, "I think I fucked up."

"Fucked up what? What happened?"

Champagne went on to tell Candy about how she didn't trust her best friend's boyfriend. She told her how, unbeknownst to Zyair, she and Thomas went to a swingers club to catch him fucking up and ran into her ex-boss.

In the process of telling this story, Champagne had a couple more shots of Patron and was feeling quite nice. "Anyway, Zyair found out because Jackson came into his restaurant and caused a scene. This whole thing has become a mess, and I don't know what to do about it."

While Champagne was in a talking mood, Candy decided to ask her about the time she and Zyair was in Ladies First. "So what's up with you and Zyair coming to the 'ladies bar'?"

Champagne figured, *To hell with it*. "We were looking to do something different."

"Something like what?"

"Why are you so curious?"

"I just am. I know that most couples go to the clubs looking to get into something."

Champagne didn't bother answering. She stood up and said, "Maybe I should go to my room and call Zyair."

Candy stood up also. "I don't know if it's a good idea for you to call him when you're in this condition."

Champagne felt herself tilt a little to the left. "You know what, maybe you're right. Maybe I should wait until the liquor wears off. I think I'll go to my room and lay down."

"How about I walk you to your room? I don't think you're going to make it on your own."

Champagne looked Candy in the eyes. "That just might be a good idea."

CHAPTER TWENTY-NINE

"IT'S ECSTASY WHEN YOU LAY DOWN NEXT TO ME"

BARRY WHITE

Zyair was in his office, his head in his hands, when DaNeen approached him.

"Are you okay?"

Looking up, he told her, "As okay as I can be."

DaNeen walked around his desk and started massaging his shoulders. "Do you want to talk about it?

Everything in Zyair knew he should ask her to leave, but he didn't feel like being alone. Plus, her hands felt good. "I don't know, DaNeen. Maybe I've been a fool all this time. Maybe I was living a lie with Champagne. How could I have been so stupid?" He looked up at her. "Nah, I refuse to believe that. There has to be a logical explanation. But then again, what would be a logical explanation for your boy and your woman to be at a swingers club? Can you think of one?"

DaNeen told him she couldn't, and added, "I would've never done anything like that to you. You don't need anyone like that." She turned his chair around to face her. "You need someone like me, Zyair, someone that wouldn't go behind your back with your best friend."

Zyair could feel that this was going in the wrong direction, but he needed comfort, needed to feel appreciated, something he hadn't been feeling lately. As a matter of fact, Champagne had been neglecting him. He felt like the love was one-sided, like he was the one carrying the relationship, the one using up all the energy to keep her happy and satisfied. He was tired of being taken for granted. "Even if what Thomas said is true, what the hell were they thinking?"

DaNeen didn't know what Thomas said, and she really didn't care. "I don't know, Zyair, but what I do know is, women tend to forget what they have and how good they may have it. Especially once they've gotten comfortable and in a routine with their man. I know what I'm talking about because I had a good man once and I started to mistreat him by not tending to his needs, and basically expecting and not graciously accepting. It's something I regret to this day, and I vowed to myself that the next time I came across a man that went beyond the norm, I would shower him with love and affection."

Zyair liked what he was hearing. He wanted to be showered with love and affection. He didn't want to be treated as an afterthought. "Damn, girl, that sounds good."

"I have something that will feel just as good." DaNeen didn't wait for an answer. She bent down and placed her lips on his. She waited for him to respond, and when he did, she sat on his lap.

In the back of his mind, Zyair was telling himself to stop, but the hurt in his heart was urging him on. He turned her around so that she was straddling him.

"Is the door locked?" he asked her.

DaNeen stood up and went to check. It wasn't, so she locked it.

Zyair stood up, and together they moved towards the chaise. Zyair sat down, and DaNeen stood in front of him and slid her skirt down.

Zyair was surprised to find that all she wore underneath was stockings and a garter belt.

She leaned over and unbuckled his belt.

He stood up, and together they pulled his pants down.

DaNeen lay back on the chaise, and Zyair climbed on top of her. There was no foreplay, no kissing, no caressing.

They looked each other in the eyes, and DaNeen, still seeing the hurt on his face, told him, "It's okay. I've been wanting this for a long time."

Zyair placed his hands under her ass and pulled her into him real hard. He did this a couple of times, until he heard her wince. After realizing that it wasn't DaNeen's fault that he was hurt, he decided to slow down his pace.

She understood what he was doing and allowed him to have his way with her. However he wanted her, she'd give herself to him. If he wanted to fuck her hard, she'd let him. If he wanted to make slow, passionate love to her, she'd let him.

Zyair was in a daze. He was well aware of what he was doing and knew he was in the wrong. He thought doing this would make him feel better, but it didn't. As a matter of fact, it made him feel worse because he wasn't that kind of man and he was operating outside himself. He was operating off his emotions.

Deep down, he knew Thomas and Champagne wouldn't mess around with one another behind his back. He also knew that Champagne had been bugging over the whole Khalil and Alexis relationship. He could see her doing something as stupid as going to a swingers club to get evidence. He was just pissed off by the deception and being left out of the loop. Especially Thomas's role.

He wondered what they saw when they were there. To him there was something intimate about that excursion.

As Zyair felt himself about to come, he realized he didn't have a condom on and pulled out of DaNeen. As he came in his hand, he wondered what Champagne was doing at that very moment.

CHAPTER THIRTY
"SAY YES"
THE WHISPERS

Candy wanted so bad to make love to Champagne. She was laying behind her in the bed, spooning, rubbing her hair as she cried and talked.

"How could I have been so stupid?" Champagne asked. "I might have destroyed the best thing in my life by being foolish."

The Patron had Champagne telling it all. She told Candy all about Hedonism and about Sharon. "I don't know what's gotten into me. When we went to Hedonism, I had no intentions on being with a woman, but once it happened, it seemed like that's all I could think about. I used the excuse of trying it again sober to see if I liked it, and I found I did." She turned over and faced Candy. "What do you think it means? Do you think it means that I'm gay?"

Candy could see how vulnerable Champagne was feeling and wanted to take advantage of her so bad, but she knew to do that would jeopardize her job. "No, I don't think that. I think you were curious and wanted to experiment, like you said. Sometimes we need to try things more than once to see if it's what we like. You found out that you did, and I personally think it's okay to like more than one thing."

Champagne wanted to believe her. "You really think so?"

"I speak only the truth."

"Kiss me."

Although this is what Candy wanted, she was caught off guard. "Huh?"

"I said kiss me."

Candy pushed Champagne on her back and lay on top of her. "Is this you talking, or is it the liquor talking?"

"It's me talking."

"I work for you."

"I know."

"Are you going to be able to handle it?"

"All I'm asking for is a kiss."

"Nothing else?"

"Why? Do you want something else?"

Candy didn't respond with words. She responded by planting soft kisses on Champagne's lips. "Listen," she said, "if we go on with this, I want you to know I don't expect anything from you. I just want to make you feel better."

Champagne placed her hands on each side of Candy's face and said, "Stop talking and make love to me."

As Candy kissed her, she thought about Candy and Sharon, and the fact that if it had been another time and the circumstances were different, they could have seen where this would go, but because things were the way they were they couldn't. Champagne knew this was going to be it, her last time making love with a woman, and that her choice was to be with Zyair.

"Let's get undressed," she told Candy.

Candy climbed out the bed and headed towards the bathroom. "Come, follow me."

Champagne stood up and followed behind Candy to the bathroom.

Candy took two rags off the rack and told Champagne, "Let me wash you."

No one had ever offered to do that to Champagne before, and it kind of turned her on. She undressed as Candy watched and stood in front of her naked.

By now Candy had wet the rag and was on her knees. She pushed Champagne's legs apart and placed the rag on her pussy, pressing down on it. She looked up at Champagne, who was looking down at her.

"Open your legs some more," Candy told her.

Champagne did as she was instructed.

Candy then spread Champagne's lips apart and washed between her lips. She then pushed the skin back over her clitoris and wiped it gently. She replaced the rag with her tongue, sucking on it gently.

Champagne's knees buckled, and she grabbed Candy's head and pressed it against her pussy.

Candy pulled away. "I'm not done washing you yet."

Candy then took the rag and wiped from Champagne's pussy to her ass. "I'm going to lick every inch of you."

When she was done wiping Champagne, Candy went to wipe herself.

"Let me do you," Champagne offered.

"No, this is about you," Candy told her. She then took Champagne's hand and led her to the bed.

"Lay down."

Champagne did just that.

"Spread your legs wide."

Champagne did that as well.

Candy placed her knees between Champagnes legs and kneeled over her. She kissed her on the mouth. "After tonight, we're going to go back to work and pretend like this never happened."

Champagne hoped she could do that. Even if she couldn't, at this moment she would have agreed to any and everything.

Knowing that this was going to be her last girl-on-girl encounter, she pulled Candy up to her and said, "I want to taste you while you're tasting me."

"No, this is all about you," Candy told her again.

"This is your boss talking. Do what I say."

Candy laughed. "Yes, ma'am. How do you want to do this?"

Champagne said, "Sixty-nine."

"Me on top and you on the bottom?"

"However you want to do it is fine with me."

The following morning they decided to not pretend that nothing happened.

Before Candy left to go to her room, Champagne told her, "I wasn't so drunk that I don't know what happened last night."

This pleased Candy. "Good."

"Thank you."

"Anytime."

"Really?"

Candy looked Champagne straight in the eye. "Really."

When Candy left the room, Champagne knew she had to do what she'd been putting off, and that's call Zyair. She retrieved her cell phone out of her purse and dialed his cell number.

Zyair was laying in the bed when he heard his phone ring. He knew it was Champagne. She'd called numerous times that morning, but he felt too guilty about what had transpired between him and DaNeen to answer the phone.

Later than night when he arrived home, he called up Thomas and told him to stop by the following morning. He needed to hear Thomas out before Champagne arrived and before they spoke. Whatever Thomas said was going to dictate how he approached this whole situation with Champagne.

A couple hours later when Thomas arrived, they were sitting in the den, and Thomas was explaining how he and Champagne ended up at the swingers club. "Man, I know I was wrong for not telling you, but I promised her. And I know you wouldn't want her going into a place like that by herself."

Zyair was having mixed emotions about the whole thing. On one hand he wanted to fuck Thomas up again, on the other, he respected what his boy had done for him.

Thomas went on to add, "I would never do anything to jeopardize our friendship, you must know that. But like I was telling you, I'm in love with Alexis. Why? I can't even explain it, but I kid you not, man. I really think she's the one. And when I mct Khalil, and after talking to Champagne and hearing her doubts about him, I too got caught up in the moment."

By the time Thomas finished apologizing and trying to set the record straight, Zyair had made the decision to do a background check on Khalil. He just wanted to nip all this shit in the bud and move on. He also knew that in order to move on, he and Champagne were going to have to come to some sort of understanding about their relationship. Limbo wasn't working for him anymore.

He also knew he was going to have to talk to Da-Neen. He didn't want to lead her on. He knew she had feelings for him, and he wasn't the type to play on someone's emotions.

He glanced at the clock. *Yep, that's what I'll do,* he thought to himself. *I'll handle this whole situation with DaNeen, and then I'll speak with Champagne.*

CHAPTER THIRTY-ONE
"SMOOTH OPERATOR"
SADE

DaNeen was sitting in Zyair's office, listening to him apologize for the night before.

"Why are you apologizing? You didn't do anything wrong."

"I'm not apologizing for the sex. I'm apologizing for the circumstances in which the sex occurred. DaNeen, I've known for quite some time that you've had feelings for me and I have to be honest with you. I've looked forward to coming to work and feeling your energy. It boosted my ego. I shouldn't have let the other night go as far as it did, but it happened, and we have to move on."

"What the hell do you mean, we have to move on? I thought we were going to take this to the next level. Your girl and your best friend deceived you."

"Yes, they may have, but that's not a reason to start a new relationship."

DaNeen was real quiet, which made Zyair nervous. He didn't know if she was plotting something or accepting what he was saying to her.

She stood up. "You know what, Zyair, you're right. I wouldn't want you under these circumstances anyway. If there was going to be an us, I would need a whole you. I'm a big girl, and I took you any way I could have gotten you the other night and I too could have stopped it."

Zyair was impressed with the way DaNeen was handling the whole thing. "Under different circumstances, I know we could have been together."

DaNeen knew that the words coming out of his mouth were true because Zyair didn't speak nonsense and untruths. He was a standup kind of guy. She couldn't leave the room without telling him something she'd been keeping from him, especially if it meant there was a possibility of them getting together ever.

"Zyair, I need to tell you this. I saw Thomas and Champagne leaving the swingers club."

"What?"

"Let me finish. My brother is a bouncer there, and he told me that Champagne and Thomas were put out because they caused a disturbance. It appeared as if they were busting in and out of rooms."

Zyair just shook his head. "Thanks for telling me."

Then DaNeen added, "I'm giving you a verbal two weeks' notice."

"I understand."

As DaNeen was leaving Zyair's office, she spotted Champagne "ear hustling."

Stopping in front of her, she told Champagne, "Don't fuck up. I'm watching you."

Champagne didn't respond. She'd caught an earlier flight home to make a new start. Before she left Zyair's office a wedding date would be set, and no one was going to impede her plan.

Although she'd overheard Zyair and DaNeen's entire

conversation, she chose not to address it or make an issue of it. She'd created this situation, and she'd realized that in order for them to go forward, she had to leave the past in the past.

Champagne startled Zyair when she entered his office. His phone was in his hand.

He immediately hung up. "I was just going to call you. What are you doing home so soon?"

"I needed to see you. There's something I have to tell you."

"Is it about you and Thomas going to the swingers club?"

Champagne was all ready to plead her case when Zyair stopped her.

"I know what happened, and I know why. I know how crazy you are about your girl and that you would do anything to look after her, and that includes enlisting Thomas."

Champagne looked down at floor, feeling guilty. "I manipulated Thomas. I used the fact that he's in love, or thinks he's in love, with Alexis to confirm my suspicions about Khalil."

"Why are you so against this Khalil fellow?"

"I don't know, Zyair. I wish I could explain it. Maybc, it's woman's intuition."

"Well, your intuition was right."

"Huh?"

"I did a background check."

"Huh?"

"Not only is he a porno star, but he's been arrested numerous times for operating a prostitution ring."

'What?"

"He's a pimp."

"I knew it! I knew he was sheisty. That muthafucka. We need to call her right now. Oh my God, we can't."

"Why not?"

"She's in Cancun with him. They won't be back until tomorrow."

"Well, I guess we'll have to wait until tomorrow."

Champagne sat down and told him, "Have a seat. Zyair, I apologize for all I've been putting you through. I hope it's not too late for us."

"It's never too late, but you need to know we can't continue this way. Our relationship has been damaged, and I need to know that in our darkest hour we will fight, that you will fight for us."

"I will, Zyair. I will fight for us, and to prove it to you"—Champagne reached inside her purse and pulled out a small box.

"What the hell is that?" Zyair asked, jumping up.

"Sit down. You're ruining my moment."

"Uh-uh, you will not do this." Zyair went over to his desk, opened the top drawer, and pulled out a small box. "I'm the man. It's my duty to wax that booty."

They both laughed.

"Seriously though," Zyair said as he got down on one knee, "will you marry me?"

Champagne kissed him on the lips. "Yes, Zyair, I will."

CHAPTER THIRTY-TWO
"END OF THE ROAD"
BOYS II MEN

Champagne and Thomas were waiting at the airport for Alexis and Khalil to arrive. Zyair had already told them he wouldn't be far behind them, that he had something he needed to check up on.

"I'm telling you," Thomas said to Champagne, "you should let me handle this."

Champagne nudged him. "Man, we ain't trying to go to jail."

Thomas poked his chest out. "I'll go to jail for my woman."

Champagne started laughing. "Calm your ass down. This is your opportunity to be there for her."

Thirty minutes later, Alexis and Khalil were walking down the vestibule. Both parties spotted each other at the same time.

Alexis hugged Champagne. "What are you doing here?"

"Don't I get a hug?" Thomas asked.

Alexis smiled and gave him a "church hug."

"It's like that?" Thomas put his hands on his chest, feigning heartache.

"You're lucky you got that," Khalil said.

It took everything in Thomas's power not to lash out.

Champagne pulled Alexis to the side. "I need to talk to you about something."

"Well, can't it wait?"

"No, it can't."

"Whatever you have to say, you can say it in front of Khalil."

Growing impatient, Thomas exploded, "Your man is a pimp! And we got proof."

Alexis looked at Thomas and then Champagne. "You think I don't know that? That's in his past. He's saved now."

Khalil had a smug look on his face. "We ain't got no secrets. I tell my baby everything." He grabbed Alexis's hand.

"But did you tell her this?" Zyair asked as he approached with a white woman and stood behind Khalil.

Khalil turned around, and when he saw the woman, he dropped Alexis's hand.

The woman said, "I thought you were on a business trip?"

Alexis asked Khalil, "Who is this?"

"I'm his wife and the mother of his two children."

"What is she talking about, Khalil?"

Khalil ignored the question.

"Are you going to answer me?"

Busted, Khalil said, "What is there to say?"

Right then Thomas punched him in the face and sent him staggering back.

Devastated, Alexis turned to walk away, and Thomas followed close behind.

Champagne looked at Zyair. "Should I go with them?"

Zyair said, "Thomas got it."